Romantic CHOICES

PAULLETT GOLDEN
& GUEST AUTHORS

Cover Design by Fiona Jayde Media
Interior Design by The Deliberate Page
Illustrations by Doan Trang
www.fiverr.com/doantrang

Also by Paullett Golden

This compilation is dedicated to all who have faced challenging choices, choices that require courage, that could make or break a person. May you draw strength from your final decision.

A Letter to the Reader

Dear Reader,

Within these pages, you'll find a collection of short fiction, one an experimental short story by Paullett Golden featuring two different endings for the reader to choose, and four short stories written by guest authors.

The experimental short story offers the main story first, followed then by two alternate endings. The reader may choose which ending is favorable for a more personalized reading experience, or may reread the story with each ending for a double feature of juxtaposed possibilities. While this short story features only the two endings, future shorts in this series may include multiple endings with an earlier split so that each reader can decide which trope to read based on the starting plot.

The four shorts by guest authors are the contest winners of the Golden News short fiction contest. While all stories are romance, there is a combination of historical and fantasy for a varied read. The winners featured in this collection range from debut authors to seasoned authors. Be sure to check out their bios at the end of the book to learn more about them and their works.

This collection is the second of the Romantic Flights of Fancy series. All books in the series are available at printing cost only. Each release in this series alternates between an anthology of fan favorites from the Romantic Encounters series plus the inclusion of contest winning authors and an exclusive-to-series short story with multiple endings plus the inclusion of contest winning authors.

Prior to each anthology's development, a call for submissions will appear in the Golden News newsletter for those who would like to enter the contest for a chance to be published in the series. The contest is open to newsletter subscribers only. Note that the contest is for flash and short fiction only. There are many types of short fiction, ranging from micro fiction of only a few words to short stories of several thousand. Each tale within this anthology, regardless of brevity, is a stand-alone story.

You can look forward to a similar compilation of short fiction contest winners plus Golden shorts in future Romantic Flights of Fancy books.

Enjoy!
Paullett Golden

Table of Contents

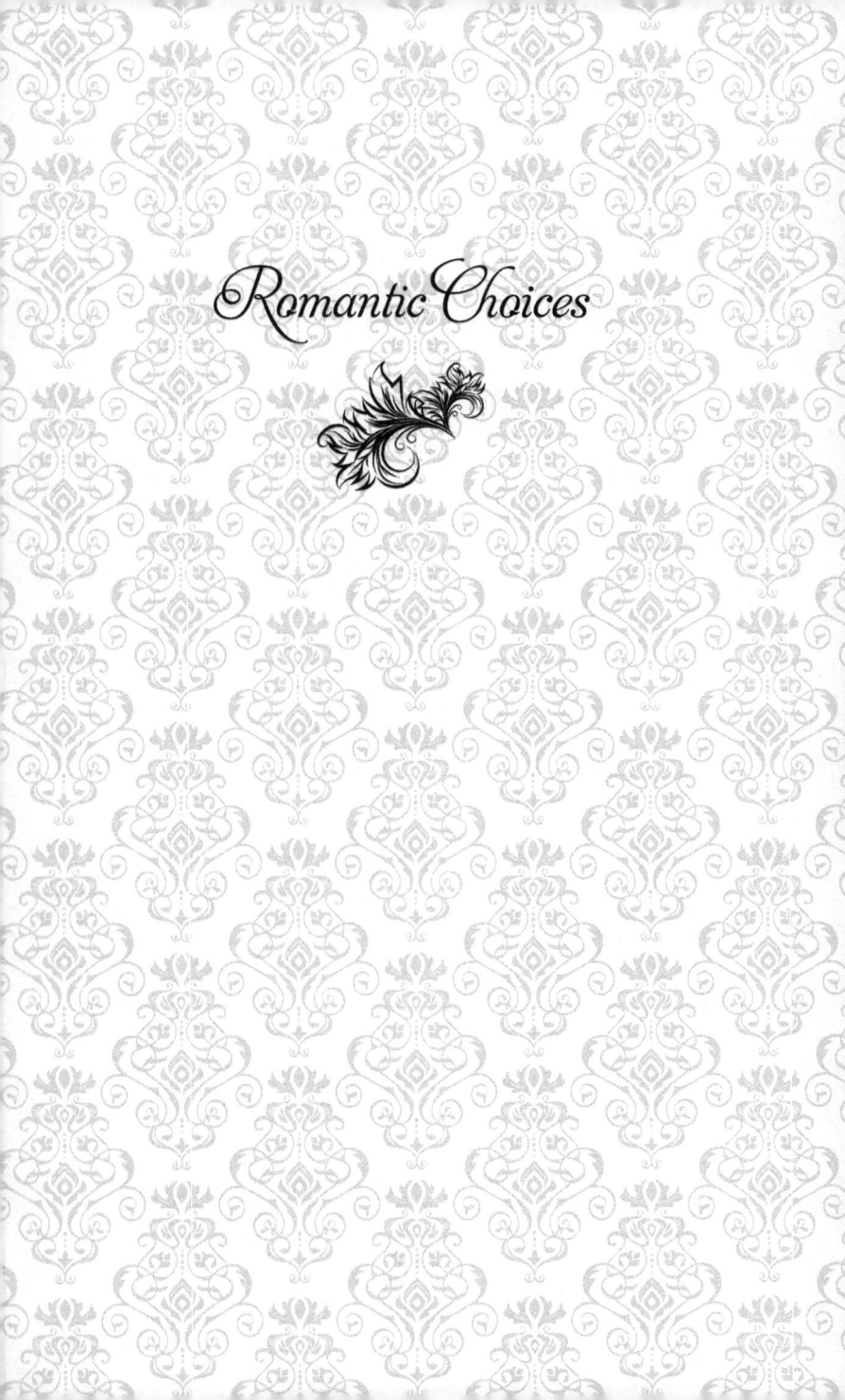

Romantic Choices

Romantic Choices

Miss Chloe Hudson nodded, schooling her features into an expression of rapt attention. Rules. So many rules of etiquette. The droning of her great aunt's voice lulled her into a stupor. Still, she nodded, her neck on a hinge.

With a clap of her hands, Aunt Caroline asked, "Now, are you ready to meet your future husband?"

Chloe's eyes widened. *Husband*? Oh dear. She ought to have paid attention. A non-committal smile should do the trick. She bared her teeth, hoping for a sparkle in her eyes that would convey, *you are the wisest of all wise aunts, and I worship your wise advice, oh wise one.*

Aunt Caroline narrowed her eyes.

Chloe smiled wider.

A toss of her gaze to the ceiling, Caroline said, "Dreaming of the garden rather than beaux. I should have known. Well, no matter. Follow my lead tonight. Pay special attention to the name *Mr. Roberts*. I shall nudge you with my elbow during that particular introduction. He's the one for you. Impeccable lineage. Incomparable income. A fine estate along Leongate's beck. Untarnished reputation. And don't forget a perfect host, namely of the annual foxhunt dating back to his great-great grandfather. Divine, yes?"

Chloe nodded again, or rather, she had not stopped nodding.

How tedious. The whole of her introduction to society had been a bore, and now this. Her eyes drifted towards the window. Sunrays shone across parterres, brightening vibrant blooms of oranges and reds. The garden begged to be walked. Yet where was she day in and day out? Stuffed in drawing rooms as her aunt made those necessary connections so important to a young lady's life.

Perhaps those connections would have been important had her family remained in York. Now, the family was in the wilds of the moors, for heaven's sake. Chloe disliked sounding ungrateful for all her aunt's help, but exchanging polite conversation with strangers could not compete with a wilderness ramble.

Her saving grace was that it was Aunt Caroline who chose to bear the mantle of Chloe's societal introduction. This and this alone filled her with hope.

Of all her aunts and great aunts, Caroline was the fun one, ten years Chloe's father's junior, despite the honorific of "great," and twice widowed, regardless of her young age. Oh, she did not have poor choice in men, nothing so terrible, rather she had a proclivity for rogues who lived daring lives outside their redemptive marriage.

Granted, Chloe did not wish for a husband who would leave her widowed, but she knew Caroline would spot a rogue amongst the honorable, and, most importantly, she would allow Chloe the freedom of choice, all while encouraging the best of gentlemen by her estimation. Or so Chloe assumed. She could trust her aunt to allow her freedom of choice, could she not?

Steepling her fingers, Aunt Caroline pressed her fingertips to her chin, "Not to stir your nerves, but everything hangs in the balance of this evening."

Chloe swallowed.

"We've made the morning rounds these past couple of weeks. All the important people know you're out, carry yourself well, and possess an admirable disposition. Now, to secure a husband." Caroline stood, waving a hand towards the drawing room door. "Up, up. I've selected a gown for the evening. The new one with the yellow trim. Your maid will be waiting."

When Chloe stood, her knees wobbled just enough to bely her excitement for the evening. All the garden daydreams in the world could not disguise her anticipation for her first dinner party. Tedious though this whole come-out business was, a first dinner party only occurred once in a lifetime — a real party!

Caroline clasped Chloe's shoulders and pulled her in for an embrace. "You'll look stunning this evening. I'll have to fight off the beaux with a sabre. Well, everyone except Mr. Roberts, of course." With a wink, she ushered Chloe upstairs.

All thoughts of wilderness walks and garden strolls shadowed in light of the dazzling dinner party. Chloe's two younger sisters and her mother would be starry-eyed over breakfast when Chloe shared her tales. She wished her mother could join, but Mama had shortened breath no physician could explain aside from offering a prescription of country air, hence their move to North Yorkshire. Chloe enjoyed the evening on her mother's behalf. The candlelight! The crowd! The conversation! All so titillating.

Upon their arrival, Aunt Caroline guided Chloe to the matrons they had called on over the past couple of weeks, each delighted to be part of Chloe's special evening. A few new introductions were made before dinner, but nearly half the guests in attendance remained a mystery. After dinner, Aunt Caroline had promised. During tea. *That* was when the best guests would attend, when the entertainment would begin, when everyone could let down their hair, so to speak — never in actuality, Caroline explained, for that would be scandalous. Although… Caroline had eyed a gentleman across the room, elbowing Chloe in the ribs. Some people might be worth a scandal, she had whispered.

When Chloe's eyes had followed the path of her aunt's, her breath hitched. Could that be *Mr. Roberts*?

All through dinner, Chloe's attention caught on that same gentleman, eager to get to the after-dinner tea when her aunt promised an introduction — *the* introduction. So, this was to be her husband. If only she could capture his attention as he had captured hers. Then, there was more to a person than a pleasing visage. It was, nevertheless, a good place to begin. Chloe sat up straighter.

However thoughtful her dinner companions to either side of her were, the delights of dinner paled to the coming introduction. Was he to be a conquest set by her aunt, or had he been nudged by a relation of his own in her direction? Not once did she notice him glance her way. Disappointing.

Her disappointment did not linger. Soon, her first ever society dinner ended, and she made the acquaintance of yet more ladies in the drawing room, followed then by the arrival of the gentlemen, tea, and pianoforte entertainment by a young lady Chloe had only just met but could not now recall by name. So many names this evening. How was anyone to remember the names to go with all the new faces?

Aunt Caroline stood sentry by her side, a hand touching Chloe's arm each time someone came into view who was a "must" to know. Chloe's hands were not so well-intentioned. They fidgeted with the length of ribbon hugging the high waist of her gown. Tug, stroke, twirl, tug. *Be still*, she scolded herself. Confidence garnered attention, not nervousness. In response to her stilled fingers, she chewed her bottom lip. No, no, no. Pursing her lips, she again scolded herself. Excitement? Anticipation? Nerves? All of these, she supposed.

A hand touched her forearm.

Chloe glanced to her aunt, who met her gaze with a slow nod. *The* nod to precipitate *the* introduction. Chloe's breath quickened.

As she turned to face the room from her strategic position next to a brightly lit candelabra — to cast a halo about her head, her aunt had explained — she saw *him* walking towards her, one of the elder ladies in attendance at his side, an elder lady who Aunt Caroline had taken Chloe to see during their morning calls no less than three times in as many weeks. Now Chloe understood why.

Viscountess Saddlerton approached, nodding first to Aunt Caroline. "It would be my pleasure to introduce my nephew, if so permitted."

Once Caroline offered her approval of the acquaintance, Chloe made free to say, "Nothing would please me more, my lady." However polite the words, Chloe could feel her cheeks warming in a blush.

Lady Saddlerton offered, "Mr. Roberts is my youngest brother's son, now the master of Ashford Park after my brother's untimely passing, God rest his soul." Angling her head to Chloe, she said, "Miss Hudson is new to Leongate, but her father's family has lived in the moors for as long as I can remember."

Her tone deepened Chloe's blush, for it seemed to say, *You'll wish to know this young lady or face my condescension forthwith*. Chloe was no one particularly special by her own account, so Aunt Caroline must have been enlivening the praise at every turn. Hopefully the praise had not overreached with promises

Chloe could not keep, such as being skilled at the pianoforte.

Mr. Roberts' bow was deep, almost reverent. When he stood to his full height, Chloe could appreciate how tall he was, far taller than he had appeared when seated at the dinner table — what a foolish thought! His attire was understated but of the finest quality silk, no question about the bespoke tailoring. A man of fine taste. Blond hair curled at the tips. Blue eyes studied Chloe, taking her measure in polite curiosity. Was that a hint of rosewater and mint about his person?

Chloe exchanged greetings. Her aunt could not have been more right about this match!

Aunt Caroline and Lady Saddlerton made a subtle step to the side to engage in conversation, leaving Chloe and Mr. Roberts to converse, all under their watchful gazes, never mind they appeared absorbed in talk about bonnets.

Mr. Roberts said, "My aunt tells me you hail from York."

Chloe twined her fingers at her waist, untwined them, then laced them behind her back, fighting the urge to fidget. Were all young ladies so nervous when meeting a prospective beau? She wished her aunt had not made it clear he was the catch of Leongate. But then, would it have made a difference? Chloe thought not. She would have liked Mr. Roberts regardless.

Smiling with an edge of shyness, Chloe said, "Yes, we've only recently let Briars Abbey — well, the manor behind the old Abbey, to be precise."

"Renting? Is your stay temporary, then?"

"We hope not. A friend of my father's offered the house, and we thought it the perfect choice while we adjust to Leongate. Should all prove favorable, we'll secure permanent lodgings, although I'm certain Mr. Timbers would let us Briars Abbey indefinitely should we wish to stay there."

Was she talking too much? Should she ask him questions instead so as not to appear too chatty?

Before she lost her courage to turn the conversation, she asked, "Am I to understand you'd recommend Leongate?"

Inane question, she realized after asking. If Ashford Park was his ancestral home, he would all too likely reside here regardless how well the village and its surrounds recommended itself. She clenched her fingers, the fussy digits still held behind her back.

Rather than raise a brow at her silly enquiry, Mr. Roberts smiled, one side of his mouth lifting in a sigh-inducing grin, his eyes softening with mirth. "If you enjoy rambles amongst the brambles, winding paths, and endless vistas of sheep-dotted moors, you're in the right place."

Her pulse raced. "Do you say that facetiously, or are you deliberately enticing me with promises of long walks?"

Now his brow did raise, although with it, his smile deepened. "I meant it however you wish to take it. Truth be told, I'm partial to those rambles, the more chance to lose my way, the better, for one never knows what one may discover along the journey."

Forgetting herself, she clasped her hands before her and laughed. "You speak my own mind, Mr. Roberts!"

"In that case, permit me to escort you and your aunt for a drive in my sociable. While neither a long walk nor an opportunity to lose our way, we could take in those vistas."

How easily was a gentleman and a young lady matched? With a single introduction, love scented the air. Chloe could not believe her good fortune.

As Aunt Caroline solidified the details of the drive with Mr. Roberts, two young ladies approached, one Chloe had met before dinner, but the other she had not been introduced to since the young lady in question had taken her post at the pianoforte to turn pages for most of the evening. Chloe's attention was then split between Mr. Roberts and the new arrivals.

The lady she knew spoke first. "Miss Hudson, I've been dying for you to meet my neighbor, Miss Tindall. The two of you are destined for friendship."

Before Chloe could respond, Miss Tindall hooked her arm around Chloe's elbow. "You're mine now. I'm determined to adopt you as my dearest friend and introduce you to all the people you ought to know. We'll have so much fun!"

Chloe gaped, her mouth forming words, but her voice speechless. A flattering introduction, but... She turned in time to see first her aunt smiling in approval, and then Mr. Roberts' expression darkening.

Arm still linked with Chloe's, Miss Tindall angled away for an exchange of whispers and giggles with her neighbor, leaving Mr. Roberts a moment to lean over to Chloe for a whisper of his own.

"Be mindful, Miss Hudson, of the company you keep," he said *sotto voce*, his tone edged with an unfriendliness she would not have thought possible only moments before.

Chloe bristled at his rudeness.

Rather than await a reply, he took his leave alongside Lady Saddlerton, not bothering to acknowledge poor Miss Tindall or her neighbor.

Miss Tindall remained unaffected by the dismissal, turning a hopeful and bright face to Chloe. "Now, we must meet all the people worth meeting. Come." She grinned at Aunt Caroline and said with cheerful enthusiasm, "I shall return her posthaste, but I claim her for at least ten minutes. I plan to make her the most popular girl in Leongate!"

Ten minutes turned into an hour. With each passing minute, Chloe liked Miss Tindall more. True to her promise, Miss Tindall introduced her to a number of young ladies and gentlemen, none of which Chloe had yet met, and all of whom were soon engaged in a lively game of charades. One particular gentleman in the group eyed Chloe enough times to give the impression he might be flirting. But with her? The first few times, she had glanced to the other side of the drawing room, hoping for a glimpse of Mr. Roberts despite her confusion over his rudeness. Not once could she spy him. After those first few times, she forgot to glance around her, enjoying the gentleman's continued attention.

As the charades turned into a card game, that same gentleman broke from the crowd to approach.

"Waste no more time. I must know her," he said to Miss Tindall, his opening words bold as brass.

Chloe's cheeks flamed.

Miss Tindall had the audacity to giggle in response. Arm still looped around Chloe's, she said, "Miss Hudson, you must forgive me. If I don't make the introduction, he'll do something ghastly like introduce himself. You should know first he is a disreputable rogue not worth knowing. Oh, yes, and a consummate gambler. I should also mention —"

The gentleman clasped Chloe's free hand and said, "Permit me to interrupt. I've been vying for an introduction all evening, but my sister was determined to ignore my request by antagonizing me at the pianoforte. Jeffrey Tindall, at your service." He bowed over her hand.

Chloe looked from Mr. Tindall to her companion. Oh! Siblings. Yes, that explained everything. Her horror of the encounter turned to amusement, then a bashful smile.

Miss Tindall teased, "See? He's an absolute terror. I would trade him for a sister any day. Will you be my sister? Now that I say it, it's too perfect not to be true. You shan't be my dearest friend, rather my sister. Jeffrey, you louse, this is Miss Hudson, my new sister. You may move out forthwith so that my new sister may move in." She giggled and tugged Chloe's arm until Chloe too was laughing.

Mr. Tindall held fast to Chloe's hand. "Will you partner me for the next game?"

How else was she to answer without being impolite? Of course, Chloe accepted. Aside from not wanting to appear impolite, she genuinely wished to partner Mr. Tindall. There was a vibrancy about him, a charisma that mesmerized her. He was Mr. Roberts' opposite in looks, all darkness to Mr. Roberts' lightness. That she thought of Mr. Roberts in the presence of this new gentleman surprised her, for Mr. Tindall was so intoxicating as to blur everything and everyone around her.

Late into the night, Caroline's carriage saw her and
Chloe to their respective homes. Not before Chloe
regaled her aunt with her myriad reactions throughout the evening, from anxiety to awe. The name most
on her lips was Tindall.

"Do you know the family, Aunt Caroline?"

On the tip of her tongue was to ask if he was a suit-
able beau, but she could not assume he wished to court
her. For all his flirting, he had made no mention of calling on her. His flirting, for that matter, was not restricted
to her, as she observed during the progression of the
evening. Oh, he flirted with her boldly enough, but his
whole personality was one of teasing and amusement,
a compliment on his lips for everyone in their group at
the card table. As certain as she was he had singled her
out for special attention, she could not stake her reputation on it. And besides, what of Mr. Roberts?

Caroline was slow to respond. "I don't know the
Tindalls well. They live at the farthest end of Leongate
and align with different acquaintances than I do. Not
to say I don't favor their acquaintances, merely do not
know any of them well. Moderate estate. Mr. Tindall
Sr. favors horseracing if memory serves, and I believe
they frequent London for that purpose. Miss Tindall
seemed in earnest of your friendship, which shows
she's a young lady of good taste. I see no reason to
discourage her friendship."

Chloe glanced down at her laced fingers before
asking, "And Mr. Tindall? Her brother, that is, not
their father."

If Chloe thought her aunt was slow to respond before, it was nothing to now. They passed straight through the village before she answered.

"I don't know anything about the young man. What little I observed this evening… well, he reminds me of my first husband." She exhaled deeply before asking, "Am I to assume you preferred him to Mr. Roberts?"

Now was Chloe's turn to mull over her words. She glanced out the carriage window, but without the faint glow within the cottage windows, darkness shrouded the passing scenery.

"I enjoyed my conversation with Mr. Roberts," Chloe began at last, "and we do have the drive to look forward to, but his behavior towards Miss Tindall gives me pause."

"Mr. Roberts behaved poorly?" Caroline's pitch rose in surprise.

"A cut, to be honest. Thankfully, she did not seem to notice."

"Ah. That's unfortunate. I would not have thought it in his temperament. However disappointing, I still prefer him for you."

As the carriage reached Briars Abbey, Chloe realized she had not answered her aunt's question about whether she preferred Mr. Tindall. Did she? Had Mr. Roberts not behaved rudely, had he not whispered his cryptic warning, would she have room in her thoughts for Mr. Tindall? She could not answer. The best decision she could make for now was to look forward to the drive with Mr. Roberts. Only through better acquaintance could she answer her questions.

Chloe checked the mirror for the fifteenth time. As with each time prior, her bonnet proved straight, and her curls held. One could never be too certain when it came to the disposition of hair or clothing. They behaved of their own volition most days. *Unruly* being the temper of both in Chloe's experience.

"Stop fidgeting," Aunt Caroline said from behind her. "You're the picture of perfection."

Chloe grinned at her aunt's reflection. Try as she might to appear unaffected, she was too excited to hide her smile. The anticipation of her drive with Mr. Roberts superseded her hesitations over his behavior towards Miss Tindall. Her first drive! A gentleman was to call on her. *Her!* And not for tea and biscuits in the parlor. *A drive!* The only way this could be more divine is if there was a wilderness walk involved. Would he consider stopping the carriage at one of those scenic vistas so they might ramble amongst the brambles, as he had chided? She could but ask.

"Should I have waited until he arrived to don the bonnet?" she asked her aunt. "I don't wish to look too eager."

"Stop overthinking, and stop fidgeting. You're wrinkling your sash, not to mention you're making me nervous."

A distant knock shushed them both. Chloe strained to listen. Voices, muffled. The *thud* of a door closing. Footsteps, soft and light. Voices, more pronounced. Footsteps, heavier, more prominent. Chloe strangled her sash. Indisputably the sounds were drawing closer to the parlor. Her smile faltered as she looked to her aunt for strength. Her first drive with a gentleman.

The parlor door opened, and the butler stepped in to announce Mr. Roberts. Both Chloe and Caroline stood in welcome.

If possible, he was more handsome than he had been at the dinner party. Windswept hair, a gleam in his eyes, his cheeks rosy from the drive. No signs of the shadowed scowl from their previous parting. His lips bore a smile that shortened Chloe's breath.

"Good afternoon, Mrs. Riley, Miss Hudson. Are you both ready for a spirited drive to one of the highest points in the moors? I've my eyes set on Blakey Ridge, only a few miles north, but it should make for a memorable drive."

Aunt Caroline tied the ribbons of her bonnet. "Don't judge me too harshly when I say I've never been. Shocking, I know, when we live so near."

"Then you're in for a treat, Mrs. Riley. I've a proposition if I can tempt you both. There's an inn at the peak, rumored to have been built by monks in the sixteenth century. While the crowd is of the trading variety, they have some of the best fish west of Scarborough."

Chloe tried to suppress her squeal of delight. *Tried* being the operative word. Mr. Roberts' full attention turned to her, a mischievous grin replacing his smile.

"There's a caveat," Mr. Roberts said to Chloe. "We would have to walk there. Amidst the brambles."

Chloe's *ooh* escaped as eagerly as her squeal. Had she ever wanted to fool Mr. Roberts into thinking her a staid lover of drawing rooms and genteel conversation, she was ruining her chances.

Mr. Roberts continued, clearly fueled by Chloe's glee. "The carriage can take us as close as three miles, but from there it's traversable only by feet and livestock."

Aunt Caroline spoke then, or rather, she shrieked. "Three miles? Uphill, I presume? It could *rain*."

They all turned towards the parlor window, a cloudless sky enticing them.

"Oh, auntie, where's your sense of adventure? If I could have but a moment to change my shoes, I'll race you both to the carriage."

Not the most ladylike words or behavior, but if Mr. Roberts wanted someone weak spirited, he should learn of her disposition sooner rather than later. Nothing sounded more splendid to her than a walking adventure—across the moors, no less! When else would she have this chance? As she ascended the stairs to her bedchamber, leaving her party in the parlor, she wondered if one could fall in love with a gentleman based on an invitation to walk the moors.

That her aunt was humoring her proved just how favorable Mr. Roberts was by Caroline's estimation. Chloe did not doubt her aunt had assumed a "drive" entailed a carriage ride from Briars Abbey through the village, and then back. If Caroline was not wishing for rain, Chloe would be shocked.

When she descended again, the butler directed her to the front hall. Caroline and Mr. Roberts had removed outside to the carriage. Containing her desire to skip to the door tested her mettle.

Her attention on the promise of the day, the expectant visage of Mr. Roberts, and the welcoming spring air, she almost missed the two people standing with her aunt. It took long moments to deliberate, moments in which she should have approached, should have fixed a warm smile, should have... something. Instead, she stood on the first of three steps leading to the front door, staring, head tilted in confusion.

Mr. and Miss Tindall were chatting with her aunt.

Mr. Roberts was exchanging words with his driver.

Mr. Tindall's arm was hooked over the carriage door, his laugh filling the courtyard. Miss Tindall held her hand to Caroline's forearm, sharing the laugh from whatever Chloe's aunt had said. Chloe glanced around. No other carriage was in sight, only Mr. Roberts' sociable. In this suspended moment, she felt the conflicting tug of emotions, one part pleased to see her new friends and flattered by Mr. Tindall's marked attention to have called on her — or so she assumed was his intention — but then one part panicked to have her drive with Mr. Roberts delayed. She knew not what to do.

Her aunt spotted her and waved her over. "Aren't you popular today, Chloe? Look who has walked here from the Crawford's."

Miss Tindall slipped her hand into the crook of Chloe's elbow. "We wanted to surprise you. I'm relieved we weren't ten minutes later, or we would have missed you. Miss Crawford is a dear friend of mine, you know, and I oft call on her, but then I thought, if I were to see her, why not see you, as well? When Mr. Tindall heard my plan, he insisted on joining me, the beast. Can you believe I've been stuck with his company all morning?"

Mr. Tindall afforded Chloe an appreciative perusal before saying, "If we had suspected you might like a drive, we would have brought the gig. Left it at Crawford's place, seeing no reason to take it when it's a short walk here. You like a drive, then? Shall we send a man to fetch the gig? It would be my pleasure to take you for an unforgettable ride, Miss Hudson."

"Don't be silly, Jeffrey," Miss Tindall scolded. "The gig only has two seats. Where would I sit?"

Chloe looked to her aunt and then to Mr. Roberts before saying to the Tindalls, "Thank you for calling on me, but I'm unable to invite you inside. Mr. Roberts has already offered to take my aunt and me for a drive to Blakey Ridge."

Mr. Tindall tutted. "Hardly appropriate for the ladies. Harsh terrain, scorching sun — when it isn't raining. What's the prize? Nothing there but an inn fit for cockfights. Why don't we all drive to the old priory in Rosedale, see the ruins? Not far, closer than Blakey, and we needn't leave the carriage."

Miss Tindall piped in, "What a brilliant idea, Jeffrey! Sometimes, but only sometimes, I'm not ashamed to admit you're my brother." Reaching a hand to touch Aunt Caroline's arm, she said, "You may stand down, Mrs. Riley. We'll serve as Miss Hudson's chaperones. Between the two of us, we'll ensure not a single private moment is allowed between Miss Hudson and Mr. Roberts." She tittered at her own words.

As happy as an outing with friends sounded to Chloe, she was uncertain Mr. Roberts would take too kindly to the suggestion. Having Mr. Tindall present complicated matters further. She had been hoping for at least one private moment with Mr. Roberts. How else was she to become better acquainted with him?

Rather than allow her to have a say in the matter, the Tindalls pleaded with Aunt Caroline, who did not need much persuasion since she had, she confessed, not been eager to march across the moors, but had agreed for Chloe's benefit. With relief, Caroline relinquished her seat in the carriage to the Tindalls. Mr. Roberts bore an open frown of displeasure at the change. For the length of three breaths, Chloe expected him to bow out, perhaps not to renew his offer for a drive, but on the fourth breath, he nodded and offered to help both Miss Tindall and Chloe into the sociable carriage, his expression shielded, his movements stilted.

Determined to be optimistic about all the fun they would have as friends on an outing, Chloe considered it fortunate the Tindalls joined them, for surely once they all frolicked together across the moors or ruins or wherever they were going, they would all become the best of friends.

With Chloe and Miss Tindall facing the gentlemen, whose backs were to the horses, they had uninterrupted views to all sides. So help her, she would one day have an open carriage of her own. Brilliant invention! Nothing blocked the sunrays or shielded the wind. The passing scents of floral nature combined with sheep energized her.

"Here we are," Mr. Tindall said, waving an arm towards forgotten stones stacked in the semblance of a mostly dismantled priory — to be fair, a chapel wall and one tower still stood, but in sad disrepair. "I wager they'll repurpose these stones one day. A shame to leave them sitting around unused. Use the stones to build something useful, I say, be it a new church, housing, or otherwise."

"I hope not," Chloe protested. "They're an important feature of the landscape now, a living history, really, of what once was. Look how nature has reclaimed them." She admired the heath and gorse flourishing around the stones, moss of some variety growing along the sides of weathered rock. "Shall we explore?"

"Preposterous." Mr. Tindall scoffed. "The point was to admire from the safety of the carriage. Bad enough you both are being exposed to the deadly rays — can't have those gloriously ivory complexions darkened, can we? Think of your safety, Miss Hudson. You could take a tumble. Perfectly viewable from here, don't you agree?"

Twirling her parasol, Miss Tindall said, "Jeffrey's correct, of course. He always is, however vexing. Best to admire from the carriage."

Chloe pressed her back against the seat. As breathtaking as the view, what was the point to sit and admire without physical connection? She wanted to feel the earth beneath her soles, press her palm to the mossy rocks — would she be touching the same place where a centuries-past monk or nun once touched?

The thought thrilled her. Could they enter the little circular tower, stand at the top to imagine what the priory once looked like, take in the views?

She turned to Mr. Roberts, who, for all his exuberance to take her for a drive, had spoken nary a word since leaving Briars Abbey. Instead, Mr. Tindall had shared tales aplenty, keeping conversation alive and laughter in abundance, at least between the ladies. Now, she turned to Mr. Roberts for his support. If he would agree with her, the two could explore the ruins while the Tindalls remained in the carriage. Despite the bright sun, his expression was shadowed. He looked back at her with all the grim solemnness of a man in mourning.

She sighed. Was he so ill tempered?

There was no one to second her motion to explore, then. While this was not Blakey Ridge, a hike to an inn with fish as the culinary gem, or a remote drive through the moors, it was as close as they would get with the Tindalls joining the party. Why waste a good outing? With a deep breath, Chloe unlatched the carriage door and leapt out before anyone could stop her. Leaving behind her companions' exclamations and her own gleeful laugh, she made straight for the old priory, her half-boots primed for adventure, namely scaling rough-hewn stone and traversing overgrown brush that snagged at the hem of her travel cloak.

More stone was scattered than stacked, the only signs of historical architecture the tower and the single chapel wall, distinguished by the shapes of lancet windows. Chloe did not wish to rush her tour. The concern of being ushered back to the carriage quickened her steps, nonetheless.

She did not stop until she reached the entry to the circular tower. A single doorway, squat and square, led to an open room, a circular stair, crumbled along the ground floor, wound to a floorless first story, the top of the tower open to the sky, only a few stones at the top remaining to reveal a possible second story or roof. So small inside, only two people, perhaps three in a squeeze, could fit. Ambitious ivies and brush stole through the cracks in the stone. What she had thought to be a tower was nothing more than an old stairwell, not that it detracted from the excitement of historical importance or natural beauty, and technically, she supposed, it was still a tower, but she had thought it might be a hint to life at the priory. A shame she could not climb the stairs. Too crumbled, too many stones missing.

As she dipped under the doorway to investigate the chapel wall, she collided with a human wall. Tall, broad, as solid as the stone beneath her feet. She gasped and took a step back.

"Oh, it's you," she said, her words little more than a breathy whisper.

The corners of Mr. Roberts' lips twitched. "Disappointed?"

In a stuttering laugh, as breathy as her greeting, she said, "On the contrary."

They stood, staring at each other, for so long it should have been awkward. Just as she had said to him, any awkwardness was quite contrary. She tilted her head at his frown and smiled. In slow time, he returned the smile. Taciturn to friendly in a few deep breaths.

"It's a Cistercian Priory," Mr. Roberts explained. "Nestled in the dale, surrounded by moors, a group of nuns — yes, nuns, not monks in this case — lived as self-sustained sheep farmers for four centuries, and more than likely would have continued to do so if given the choice. Do you like ruins as much as rambles?"

Chloe leaned a shoulder against the sturdy stone of the doorway, secretly hoping it was, indeed, sturdy. "Yes and no. I like exploring. Full stop. Be it nature, history, or otherwise. I would prefer a hike along the ridge, I believe, but that is a betrayal to all this priory offers. Is it no less worthy of our appreciation?"

Tugging her bottom lip between her teeth, she fretted he would find her peculiar. One did not win a husband by tearing dress hems on bushes and clambering stone, much less personifying ruins and paths.

Mr. Roberts made to say something, stopped himself, rubbed the back of his neck, then said, "The Stemfords are hosting a soirée next week. I'm certain your aunt will have secured an invitation. I'll be there. Dancing is almost a certainty. Not a single one of their soirées has ended without the rug being rolled before the end of the night."

"Are you asking me to dance?"

"Only if you intend to say yes."

Heart thumping and knees knocking at the direction of the conversation, Chloe parted her lips to affirm, but was interrupted by the shrill laughter of Miss Tindall as she approached with her brother. Mr. Roberts bowed his head in parting, then excused himself to return to the carriage without a word of greeting to the Tindalls. Chloe could not make out his behavior. One minute kind, almost teasing, and the next ill-tempered and bad mannered.

Miss Tindall walked around the tower, chatting to no one in particular about the unpleasant overgrowth, as Mr. Tindall took Mr. Roberts' place.

He rested a hand against the stone exterior and leaned towards Chloe. "We must make the best use of this private moment." With a grin Chloe could only describe as wicked, and with eyes hooded, he said, "Run away with me."

Chloe chocked on her half laugh and half gasp. "I beg your pardon, Mr. Tindall."

"I guarantee it would be more adventurous than a pile of rocks."

"It was your idea to come to the priory, need I remind you?"

"I wasn't talking about the ruins." He leaned closer.

She was slow in understanding his meaning. Even as she deciphered the words, she was not certain she had discerned correctly. The metaphor was... Mr. Roberts?

The musk of his cologne dizzied her senses.

"I jest, Miss Hudson. All to see you smile. Well, if you had agreed, then I would claim my proposal earnest."

His pitch so low, his voice so soft, his chuckle so throaty, Chloe felt his words more than heard them, the world around her blurring as it had during the dinner party. Had she not just been talking with Mr. Roberts about dancing? Had Miss Tindall not just stood feet from the tower door, laughing over a joke Chloe had not heard? She could not recall, could not focus. Mr. Tindall's presence was all consuming, all encompassing. Trapped in the doorway of the tower stairwell, she felt one part smothered by his closeness and one part enraptured.

"Permit me," Mr. Tindall continued, "to make an observation." With liberties he had not been granted, he reached up to toy with one of the ringlets escaping her bonnet. "You have limitless potential. Like a bud waiting to bloom. With the right guidance, you could blossom. Have you thought of using rouge? Just a touch here..." He feathered his fingertips across her cheeks. "And here..." A caress to her lips. "How exquisite you could look, my dear."

Chloe's breath had caught in her throat. She remained still, paralyzed in place, uncertain how to respond. Scream? Laugh? Blush? She was torn between running to the safety of the carriage or falling into Mr. Tindall's arms. If only she could think. A fog of heady cologne and velvet words clouded her mind.

"Think how beautiful you could be by embracing your assets rather than hiding them."

Only when he tugged at the fichu around her neck did she realize he was not talking about her complexion.

"Jeffrey!" called Miss Tindall. "Stop monopolizing Miss Hudson. She's *my* friend, not yours. Or rather, she's *my* sister, not yours."

Undaunted, Mr. Tindall leaned in so close, Chloe could feel his breath against her cheek. "Thank God for that."

In a single blink, sunrays blinded Chloe, and a gust of wind chilled her. She drank in the fresh air as though parched. Two blinks to reorient herself. Up ahead, the Tindalls linked arms and made their way back to the carriage where Chloe assumed Mr. Roberts waited. A saving grace there was not a direct line of sight from the carriage to the tower doorway.

She glanced to the chapel wall. It would have to remain unexplored for today.

Before setting out for the soirée, the Hudson family gushed over Chloe's transformation. The compliments delivered her into the Stemford home on a wave of confidence.

For a week, she had pondered Mr. Tindall's words about having potential. The words had more of an effect than he perhaps intended. She tried to see herself through his eyes only to discover how immature he must think her. Romping around ruins? Marching over moors? Hiding under layers of modest fashion? Baring delicate skin to the sun? Here she was, out in society, enjoying the spring entertainments alongside those neighbors who did not partake in the London Season, but doing so as her old self, as the naïve girl she once was. Now was the time to become the adult she ought to be, the woman she could be.

She pursed her lips, hoping the rouge was not too dark.

Aunt Caroline, standing next to her in the receiving line, frowned. Of everyone in the family, her aunt had been the only one not to offer a compliment at the transformation. Rather than express disapproval, she had merely asked Chloe, *Why*? The answer could not be expressed in a single carriage ride, so Chloe opted for a shrug and secretive smile.

They made short work of the greetings before beginning their promenade around the perimeter of the room, taking in the frivolity and exchanging pleasantries with those they knew. The dancing had not yet begun, but Chloe could spy a number of guests strolling the garden outside. She itched to join them. It had rained every morning for the past week, including this morning, leaving little time to enjoy the fine spring weather. This evening was perfect.

Trying not to bite her lip lest she muss the rouge, she reined in her desire to rush outside. A woman reaching her potential preferred indoors, after all. Gardens were meant to be admired from a window. She searched the room. What would Mr. Tindall think of her transformation? Would he see the bloom?

Aunt Caroline nodded across the room. "Lady Saddlerton is here. I don't see Mr. Roberts, though. He may be in the garden or the card room."

Chloe's pulse quickened at his name. Inexplicably, she blushed with self-consciousness. As proud as she was to be reaching her potential as a society woman, the low neckline of her décolletage, along with the absent fichu she favored, had her wanting to hide from him. Preposterous reaction. He would recognize that bloom Mr. Tindall had alluded to. He would be so taken with her, he would demand a duel from any other gentleman who sought her affections. Regardless of how he ought to react, Chloe's hands hovered at her neck as if to hide her exposed flesh.

Any second thoughts were soon dashed after more compliments on the styling of her dress, the curl of her hair, and the rose in her cheeks.

"Miss Hudson!" called a voice.

Caroline and Chloe both turned to see Miss Tindall sidestepping guests to reach them.

"Good evening, Mrs. Riley. You may stand down. She's in good hands now."

If her aunt planned to protest, as Chloe thought she might since the hunt for Mr. Roberts was still afoot, she had no occasion to do so, for Miss Tindall clasped Chloe's arm and dragged her away before her sentence ended.

"Don't you look marvelous this evening, Miss Hudson. Although..." Miss Tindall eyed Chloe askance as they left the drawing room behind and entered a smallish library. "Have you considered cutting your hair? All the fashionable ladies in London wear their hair short. Besides, the curl holds better. Have I mentioned how frequently we go to London? We would be there now except Papa is convalescing from an injury. Minor but inconvenient. We never miss London in the spring. Ah, here we are. Sit next to me."

Tugged into a chair, Chloe took in the scene. The library had been designated as the card room for the evening. Ten or so other guests gathered around a table where a game of some sort was underway. She noticed three things in quick succession. The guests were notably highbrow. The glasses were full, and not with lemonade. Mr. Tindall was one of the players, his attention on a two-column line of cards.

Miss Tindall angled to whisper, "He's won two games in a row so this round he has staked his best horse."

"They're making real wagers?" A foolish question fit for a naïve girl. This did not look like a crowd to wager only chips.

Miss Tindall did not answer, her eyes riveted on the table.

A gentleman clutching a quizzing glass flipped over a card from his deck. In response, the other players placed a chip on one of the columned cards. Except Mr. Tindall. He studied the table for an eternity before he made his move, selecting the nine of spades. The gentleman with the quizzing glass turned over two cards. The crowd murmured. A sweep of the gent's hand and he collected all chips except Mr. Tindall's, instead, adding a matching one atop the stack.

Miss Tindall pinched Chloe's forearm. "Three in a row, and he's now one horse wealthier."

Chloe raised her eyebrows, continuing to watch as a new game began. She had never played faro, but she knew of it. Could serve her well to learn the rules if the Tindalls enjoyed playing.

Not halfway through the next game, Chloe stifled a yawn. A glance around the library led to disappointment. No windows to admire the garden or judge the passage of time. Were they to stay in the library much longer? She did not want to miss the dancing and longed for conversation. The game continued. Chloe waited, fighting the flutter of her eyelashes from boredom.

A guffaw from one of the guests startled her back to reality. All around her, the guests began to stand, shake hands, talk, refill drinks, and mill about the room while the gentleman with the quizzing glass swapped tables to prepare for a different game. A giggle next to her stole her attention.

"He's finally spotted you," Miss Tindall said, nodding to her brother.

Mr. Tindall moved from the table towards them, taking Chloe's measure in a deliberate and appreciative sweep of his eyes. As he took Chloe's hand in his to bow over it, he gazed up at her with those hooded eyes she could not forget.

"Delicious," he murmured, letting the word linger before adding, "is the evening's brandy. Allow me to retrieve a glass for you."

"Oh, no, but thank you," Chloe hastened to say. "I would prefer…" She hesitated, then, the word *lemonade* caught between her lips. Was she not supposed to be blossoming into a mature woman, reaching her potential? How childish to ask for lemonade. But she despised alcohol of any kind. The smell, the taste, the everything nauseated her.

"Sherry?" he asked, arching a dark brow. A nod to a heretofore invisible footman had a slender glass of sherry produced before Chloe could protest.

She could hold it, could she not? Hold it without imbibing, then slip it somewhere inconspicuous when he was not looking.

"Your sherry, Miss Hudson," Mr. Tindall offered, his fingers caressing hers as she accepted the glass. "Nothing would make me happier than to see those rouged lips kiss the liqueur."

If her cheeks did not match the liquid, she would be shocked, but then, how could anyone tell when her cheeks were as rouged as her lips? Her confidence faded. She wanted nothing more than to stroll the garden, talk about Cistercian Priories and inns with the tastiest fish west of Scarborough, and wear her half-boots topped with a modest fichu.

Swallowing against the lump in her throat, she tipped back the glass, grimaced past the acridly sweet sin, and tried to embody the fashionable and sophisticated woman she was so determined to emulate this evening.

Crinkles formed to either side of Mr. Tindall's eyes as his smile broadened. "I claim you for the evening. You'll be my lady luck. Sit with me by the table."

Chloe looked from Miss Tindall to her brother. "I would love to, but I've already overstayed. I ought to see to my aunt and, and, and I've promised at least one dance."

Slipping a hand beneath her elbow, Mr. Tindall pulled her gently towards him. "Nonsense. You're mine this evening. My sister will assure your aunt that we'll see you home. The games are certain to continue until dawn, and I won't let you leave my side until I've won every game."

"Dawn!" Chloe could have choked on the word. She normally rose at dawn to best take advantage of the day, never to miss a moment of daylight, the sunrise her morning companion. Not to return home until dawn?

Ignoring her, he said, "Come, I wish to introduce you to a few friends." As he guided her to the other side of the library, leaving his sister behind, he leaned down, his breath close enough to tickle the tip of her ear. "You're a remarkable lady when you show yourself to advantage. I believe I'm now experiencing a taste of the woman you were destined to become."

For how long she remained in the card room, she could not begin to guess. Hours, days, lifetimes. Try as she might to extricate herself, she could not find a viable excuse convincing enough for Mr. Tindall. Worse, she enjoyed his attention. Between each round of whatever game he played at the time, he whispered compliments, promises of all she could become, hints to how well she might look in a certain color or cut. She would not say he made her feel pretty so much as he convinced her she *could be* pretty. No, more than pretty. A stunning beauty. A breathtaking goddess. With the right styling, a little more rouge, the right color, a little lower bodice, more sherry, she could be the most exquisite woman of his acquaintance. The time passed in a daze for Chloe, one filled with promises, murmurs, and stomach-knotting chuckles.

Had Aunt Caroline not come for her, she may have stayed until dawn.

Miss Tindall tried her best to convince Caroline that Chloe was in good hands, but as Caroline retorted, that was rather the point — she was in a gentleman's hands of which she was not betrothed. Chloe could have swooned had she not been made of sterner stuff. Mr. Tindall, in truth, had an arm draped around her during his current game, but no one in the card game had noticed, and in fact, neither had Chloe aside from experiencing that strange lightheadedness around him, a combination of sherry and his cologne, no doubt. Yet there she was with a gentleman's arm about her. At least it was only Aunt Caroline to have witnessed. But still. Aunt Caroline had witnessed! Chloe was mortified.

As Aunt Caroline escorted her from the card room back into the drawing room where the dancing was well underway, the harpsichord plucking a lively minuet, and everyone appearing to be having a gay time, Caroline hissed, "Silly, reckless, senseless. I don't blame you, but you must be cautious. I've lost my trust in Miss Tindall, and I see now why Mr. Tindall reminds me so much of my first husband. I'll not forbid you from seeing them, as they are a respectable family, but I urge caution."

"Yes, auntie," Chloe said, head bowed, chastised and wounded.

"I have only myself to blame. This is my task as chaperone and sponsor. Blame me but heed my warnings. However sincere his attentions — which is debatable — I do not believe he is a good match for you."

Chloe could not disagree. That did not dissuade her thoughts, most of which were still in the card room, being lovingly caressed by tender fingers and brandy-scented exhales.

Distracted, she followed her aunt around the perimeter of the room until they stopped near an opening that offered foremost a clear view of the dancefloor but also a cooling breeze. The sun had long since set. Chloe could not make out anyone strolling the garden anymore. At least the breeze refreshed her.

Not until the chilly air prickled her clammy skin did she acknowledge how stuffy the card room had been.

One glance at the dancers had her pulse racing. Mr. Roberts paired a dainty girl with sooty lashes. After a pinch of jealousy that squeezed her heart, she sighed aloud to see him. He was... angelic, all blond and fair lightness with an open expression and a modest suit of celestial blue with floral embroidery. He danced impeccable figures, a partner for whom to vie. Had she missed her dance with him? They had not set a specific dance, though. Had he noticed her missing from the room all this time? However innocent was her time in the card room, surrounded by others, including Miss Tindall, she could not stop the pang of shame. There was nothing wrong with her behavior. She had not behaved badly. So why did she feel as though she had? Her eyes burned, and her throat constricted. To distract herself, she gazed out the window, thankful it was open to the night so she could not see him in the reflection of the glass.

Two full dances passed, both of which Mr. Roberts partnered with someone else. Chloe remained at her aunt's side, chatting casually with those who approached, but otherwise sat out each dance. Had she stayed in the drawing room, she was positive she would have danced every set. At this point in the evening, all dances would have been asked and accepted. How disappointing. She had never danced before. It had been the allure of the evening — that and Mr. Roberts. Dancing, at last! She knew how to dance, of course, as she practiced often with her sisters and even with her father, but outside of family evenings, she had never danced with a real partner at a real

party. This was not a ball. It was far better. It was a
lively, country party wherein the guests insisted upon
closing the day with a reel.

As it dawned she had missed the dancing and
Mr. Roberts' company, that very gentleman appeared
before her. She had not seen him approach. Her hand
fluttered to her neck as her breath caught.

"Mrs. Riley, Miss Hudson." He greeted them both
before offering a hand to Chloe. "We've saved the
best dance for last."

They were to dance after all! So giddy she did
not hide her enthusiasm when she accepted his hand,
offering a smile in return. He guided her to the center
of the drawing room where, as he had predicted, the
rug had been rolled out of the way and the furniture
moved aside, not a large space but enough to accom-
modate a couple of sets. The music began, and her
feet responded on command.

Dancing with Mr. Roberts was effortless. A superb
lead, he guided, supported, and encouraged. The figures parted them, united them, parted them again, yet
in every parting, there was an invisible thread connecting Mr. Roberts with his partner, entwining the
two throughout the dance. Chloe was aware of him
even when facing someone else in the line or clasping
hands with another gentleman for a spin. Conversation flowed, as effortless as the dancing, him asking
after her family, curious about her sisters, her mother's
infirmity, the joy of living at Briars Abbey. More than
once he circled to how well they found Leongate — well
enough for a permanent home, or still too early to say?

If she thought he would part after the dance
ended, she was mistaken. He led her across the room,

as though to return her to her aunt, only he stopped to retrieve two glasses of lemonade on the way, then offered for her to sit in one of the perimeter chairs, near enough to Aunt Caroline for propriety but far enough for a private conversation. Although the dancing was at an end, theirs being the last of the evening, the guests were too spirited to leave, everyone loitering to talk further.

"Is the lemonade to your liking?" he enquired, nodding to her glass. "I thought the coolness would quench us after the exertion of the dance, but if you'd prefer tea or even coffee...."

"Oh, no, please. This is perfect. It's exactly what I wanted, to be honest." She sipped, refreshed already, admiring the openness of his gaze, the featherlike lightness of his eyelashes.

"I worried you had not attended this evening. I saw Mrs. Riley but could not find you in the crowd. The garden beckoned, and I thought.... Well, I thought you might enjoy taking a turn."

Wistful, she rubbed the edge of her glass with her thumb. If only she had stayed in the drawing room instead. "I would have liked that, Mr. Roberts. Miss Tindall invited me to the card room soon after I arrived, and I suppose I lost track of time. Mr. Tindall was on a winning streak, you see."

Mr. Roberts clenched his fingers into a fist and rubbed the side of his palm against his thigh. "Yes, I see." His hand continued to iron his breeches as if to press out any wrinkles from the evening's dancing. "Be candid, Miss Hudson. Is Mr. Tindall courting you?"

Chloe leaned away, taken aback by the question, not only the bluntness of it but that she could not answer it to herself, much less to him. "I—I don't know. I believe he's taken an interest in me, but—"

"If you're considering his suit, I shall step aside. I'm not accustomed to so bold a conversation, but I feel it warranted, as I've no wish to confuse either of us, not after seeing you so altered this evening."

Chloe pinched her brows. "Altered? Because I was in the card room?"

He shook his head. "*You*. You're altered. I would not have recognized you had you not been standing with Mrs. Riley. You… you… I've not the words."

"You're pleased?"

His grimace said what his words could not. "Why would you change to be something you're not?"

She straightened her posture. Was he insinuating she did not have potential, that she could never be someone greater? Her chin quivered, but she could not say if it was from anger or upset.

"I thank you for the dance, Mr. Roberts, and the lemonade. If you'll return me to my aunt, I would be grateful."

His hesitation had her heart hammering, as though he would insist on insulting her further, but at the end of his silence, he stood, offered her his hand, and led her the short distance to her aunt before wishing them both a good evening.

Chloe plucked a blade of grass. Smooth, velvety, earthy aroma. She wrinkled her nose to keep from sneezing when it tickled the skin above her lip. Twirling the blade between her fingers, she turned her attention back to the conversation.

Mrs. Green looked from face to face at those lounging on the picnic sheet around her before saying, "I favor the rhododendron walk, personally. If I might share a secret with you all…" She dipped her head as she reached for the fruit bowl. "I'm having a walk of my own installed. Be on the lookout for an invitation."

A woman with a wide-brimmed bonnet decorated in yellow flowers of some variety chortled. "Trying to outdo Mrs. Plunkett's picnic already?"

"I would never dream!" Mrs. Green waved a plum in dissention.

As frivolous as the discussion, Chloe enjoyed every word. An ancient oak's gnarled branches canopied the group, flickering a kaleidoscope of light through its leaves. Across the lawn, as well as beneath surrounding shade trees, dotted assorted groups of guests, all enjoying the newly landscaped gardens of Mrs. Plunkett.

One might assume from this description that Mrs. Plunkett was a lady of means and property. On the contrary. Mr. Plunkett was the retired gardener of Viscountess Saddlerton, and Mrs. Plunkett her former housekeeper. The Plunketts' home was little more than a quaint cottage on less than five acres, but everyone in attendance at the picnic could not help admiring how extraordinary the gardens now looked after Mr. Plunkett's handiwork, having landscaped everything himself since retirement. The only complaint was that the guests could not employ his services.

Aunt Caroline sat across from her, sampling one cake after another. Chloe stretched back, lengthening her legs before her and propping herself with palms behind her, the blade of grass twined between her fingers. If ever a fashionable aristocrat needed a hermit to reside in his landscaped hermitage, she would be hard pressed not to accept the offer. There was something about nature that called to her. That had been the trouble with her introduction to society. Everything was indoors. Every party, every tea, every call. All in a stuffy room with over-padded chairs.

Tugging at the ribbons beneath her chin, she untied her bonnet, slipped it over her chignon, and set it aside, reveling in the brisk breeze through her ringlets — which she did not doubt had already lost most of their curl, if they had not been flattened by the bonnet.

Making the rounds was Viscountess Saddlerton herself, at her side, none other than Mr. Roberts. They had not approached Chloe's group yet. For that, she was thankful. He had acknowledged her when she arrived, a polite nod of the head, but he had not spoken to her. Any thoughts of him aside from an awareness of his presence were dismissed. She would not allow melancholy to rain on so glorious a day. He had insulted her, after all. Never mind she might have deserved it after her behavior, sequestering herself in the card room for the whole of the evening as she had done.

She flicked a glance to her aunt, who favored her with an encouraging smile.

The carriage ride home from the soirée the previous week had involved a stern discussion. Oh,

Aunt Caroline had not lectured or scolded Chloe for her behavior, nothing so terrible. No, it had been far worse.

The recollection of how tightly she had clenched her fingers for the whole of the drive made her fingers ache even now.

"Let me share a tale of woe," Aunt Caroline had begun before they reached the end of the Stemford driveway. "A young lady not much older than you fell head over ears for an older gentleman, a swoon-worthy gentleman. His eyes were her undoing. Dark pools of dreams, those eyes. In them shone a world of daring, adventure, pleasure beyond one's imagining. Who could resist diving into them? Not this young lady. But there was more to the man than dreams and daring. There was a promise of something greater, something beyond the doldrums of drawing rooms, even the satisfaction of taming the feral. Can you imagine what this young lady did?"

Chloe stroked a thumb to her palm, not willing her gaze to roam forward, even knowing she would not be able to see her aunt clearly in the shadowy darkness of the carriage.

"She feared she would not be able to capture this gentleman, not someone so wild, so unreachable. And so, she did the only thing she knew she could. She compromised herself. To force his hand. A gamble, as no rogue would agree to marry a reckless maiden. As it happened, this gentleman was honorable enough to offer for her. Quite the conquest in the end, no? The beast had been leashed. What the young lady did not realize was one can never domesticate a creature of the wild. One can only cage them, and that is something no beast deserves, nor does the person holding the key to the cage."

Her knuckles throbbed. She tightened her fingers in a fist, stretched them, tightened again, laced them and curled them.

"He cannot bring you happiness, not someone like him, Chloe. If he's what you want, I'll not stand in your way, but I worry for your happiness, not to mention your reputation if he's not the honorable kind. It takes so little to ruin a young lady. An arm about the person is enough. Did you enjoy his crowd? Do you feel pretty wearing the rouge? If this is what you want, tell me honestly. Tell me this is the life you would enjoy."

Chloe had not answered. She had not needed to. The questions had not been rhetorical, and they both knew that, but Chloe had let them hang in the air between them, for her aunt knew her well enough to know the answers. Chloe wanted rambles. She wanted dirty hems and trodden boots. She wanted dances and walks through gardens. She wanted *this*, the garden picnic with the Plunketts and the Greens and the whomevers.

That did not mean she wanted Mr. Roberts or Mr. Tindall, nor did it mean she did not want either of them. She enjoyed Mr. Tindall's attention, even if it made her feel uncomfortable if not outright help- less, a cornered rabbit, for lack of a better simile. She enjoyed that he thought she had potential. She did not like his friends, however, or his means of diversion. As for Mr. Roberts, she liked him and everything he represented exceedingly well, but he had insulted her, and he had behaved rudely and with inexplicable haughtiness to the Tindalls, which was not gentlemanly behavior no matter the reason. It was all a great deal to consider.

Chloe glanced about the lawn, catching sight of Mr. Roberts leaning against a tree trunk and speaking with a group of gentlemen. Curse her traitorous heart for thumping at the sight of him.

"This look becomes you."

She squinted at Mr. Roberts, his back to her. Or at least it had been. He glanced over his shoulder, caught her gaze, then turned as quickly back to his group.

"Not that you don't carry yourself well in all styles, but you're exceptionally beautiful today."

Turning away from him in case he glanced back — she did not want him thinking she was watching him, after all — Chloe eyed Mrs. Healy to her right. To her surprise, Mrs. Healy was staring at her with an expectant expression, as though awaiting a response.

Chloe blinked twice. "I beg your pardon. Did you say something, Mrs. Healy?"

"Yes, love, I remarked on how becoming you look today. I like you better with your natural complexion. Your cheeks are naturally rosy, and the sun brightens your eyes."

Her mouth forming an O, Chloe blinked thrice more. After some thought, she asked, "But does a little rouge not enhance one's beauty?"

Mrs. Healy wobbled her head side to side, neither nodding nor shaking her head. "I suppose… more so if you're an opera singer. For you, love, I recommend your natural beauty."

"Hmm." Chloe flicked the blade of grass between her fingers.

"Don't you agree, Mrs. Riley?" Mrs. Healy asked.

Aunt Caroline raised her eyebrows, looking from Chloe to her companion.

Mrs. Healy clarified, "That Chloe looks better as she is today than she did at the Stemford soirée."

"Indubitably," agreed Aunt Caroline, raising her glass of lemonade in salute.

Giving her bottom lip a firm chew, Chloe said, "I was much complimented at the soirée. Were the compliments made in politeness or honesty?"

Mrs. Green joined in with, "You're a beautiful girl, Miss Hudson, no matter what you wear. Don't fool us into thinking your mother hasn't assured you of that, nor your looking glass."

"But," Mrs. Healy insisted, "She looks *better* as she is today."

Chloe narrowed her gaze at Aunt Caroline, wondering if her aunt put Mrs. Healy up to this.

An assent of smiling faces nodded around the picnic sheet.

Cheeks aflame from blushing, but seeing this as a fleeting chance to ask trusted friends of her aunt for candid advice, Chloe braved, "Without following the latest fashions, how does a young lady reach her potential for something greater?"

A masculine voice rumbled from behind her, "Afternoon, ladies."

Jerking to look behind her, she saw Mr. Roberts standing no more than ten feet away, his aunt with him. If she thought her cheeks were on fire before, it was nothing to now. How much of the conversation had he heard? Not until her forefinger throbbed did she realize she was strangling it with the blade of grass.

Flicking aside the plucked grass, she sat up, curling her legs to her side, tucked neatly beneath her dress.

The conversation turned with the presence of the viscountess and gentleman, everyone remarking on the garden, questioning how the viscountess could do without so skilled a gardener, and asking if Mr. Roberts had any plans for improving Ashford Park. As much as Chloe's ears perked to hear more about his home, she remained distracted by worry over how much he had overheard. Not that anything specific had been said to cause embarrassment, but it had all been rather personal. She was relieved, then, when he and his aunt departed to make the rounds to another group elsewhere in the garden. Disappointment followed, for the cozy group parted ways, as well, everyone wanting to stretch their legs, converse with acquaintances, or admire other areas of the garden.

Chloe lingered beneath the tree awhile longer before deciding she, too, wanted a stroll. Part of her missed Miss Tindall's company, neither she nor her brother in attendance, but then, on further reflection, she did not miss her friend's companionship as much as politeness dictated that she ought. Had Miss Tindall been present, she would have talked more than enjoyed the garden, leaving little time for meditation or the pleasures of birdsong. She also would have clung to Chloe before dragging her along to seek shelter in some dark corner where sunrays could not find them to cause blemishes. No, she did not miss her friend's company as much as her conscious scolded her that she ought to.

As she rounded a path leading to a vibrant display of crocuses, their violet, yellow, and ivory faces basking in the sun, she saw Mr. Roberts squatting on his haunches ahead, hands cupping the petals. Her steps halted. A glance behind her revealed she had nowhere to escape without being conspicuous in her avoidance of him. Did she want to avoid him, though? He was the one person she had hoped to see at the picnic. The person she had anticipated seeing. It was the fear he would not want to see her that gave her pause. That and the sting of his insult. Chloe swallowed her fears and approached him.

"Have you known the Plunketts long?" she asked in way of greeting.

That he did not look up at the sound of her voice proved he had spotted her before she had seen him, known it would be she who advanced rather than another guest.

"The entirety of my life," Mr. Roberts said to the crocuses. "The Plunketts worked for my aunt well before I was born. They were a familiar presence around her home, more so to a young boy who favored exploring than sitting in the nursery."

He stood, taking a moment to tug at his waist coat and flatten his coat with the palms of his hands before meeting Chloe's gaze.

"Were you a precocious child?" Chloe could not stop the smile tugging at the corners of her lips. "I can't believe it. Not you."

Angling next to her, Mr. Roberts offered his forearm and nodded for them to proceed along the path together. "Do I not seem the adventurous type? Even after proposing a hike and inn-quality fish?"

At the edges of his question hinted the unasked: *But gambling in the card room is adventurous to you?* Or so Chloe imagined.

Ignoring any hidden meaning, and ignoring the question, as well, she offered, "I'm sorry to have missed both the ridge and the inn. I did think the priory fascinating and would not mind a second viewing with more time, but I confess I had my heart set on the ramble."

Was that her attempt to solicit another invitation? Did she *want* him to call on her again? Whatever she wanted did not much matter, for he did not offer to take her on another drive.

"I, too, am sorry our plans did not go as expected," he shared. "I also must apologize for what I said at the soirée. I fear it was not received as intended."

Oh dear. He was not going to tiptoe around the insult, then. She let her hand slip from his arm and laced her fingers at her waist. Rather than reply, she admired the garden, not that she saw any of it, try as she might to focus her attention away from his words.

Mr. Roberts exhaled audibly. "It is ungentlemanly to speak so boldly, but this may be my only opportunity, as I've spied my aunt making her way towards us. Forgive my bluntness, Miss Hudson." He offered his aunt a wave in greeting just as she was delayed by another guest. "We all have choices in life, some minor, such as if we should select the veal or lamb for dinner, others more significant, such as if we should invite a young lady for a drive. From what my aunt has shared about you and your family — yes, I confess she's spoken about you — and what few conversations we've exchanged, I believe we would rub well together, well enough for me to say what I'm saying. If I know you as well as I think I do, I also believe you'll appreciate my candor."

"Mr. Roberts," she interrupted, her heart beating too rapidly to brave what else he might say.

"Please, Miss Hudson. Allow me to finish? We have so little time to talk."

Tugging at her bottom lip, she nodded.

"I don't want you to decide now or even hint the direction you're leaning. I only wish for you to consider my sentiments. I like your spirit, your enthusiasm, your eagerness to hike a ridge and climb ruins. I like *you*, Miss Hudson. What you asked me at the soirée and how you reacted to my response has plagued me since that evening. To my mind, reaching your greatest potential means becoming the best version of yourself, not becoming someone entirely different. I like who you are and the person I believe you will become if you continue to be *you* and do what you enjoy, hiking ridges and all. I apologize my words did not convey that at the soirée. I meant to compliment the person you are, not imply you were anything less."

Chloe waited for him to continue. Her bonnet ribbons bit into the tender skin beneath her chin. Her palms perspired within her gloves. Her shoes pinched her heels.

He did not continue. Several times his lips parted to say more, but each time he closed them, took a deep breath, then let silence hang between them. Not that he needed to say more. Chloe thought she understood. There was so much, though, too much, to consider, to absorb, to choose. What was she to make of all he said, all he implied?

She was saved from a response by his aunt's arrival. The viscountess accepted her nephew's arm and invited Chloe to walk with them and tell her how much she admired Mr. Plunkett's handiwork, after which, she delivered Chloe to Aunt Caroline.

Where to look first? The glittering chandeliers, candle-light reflected in the crystals? The terrace stretching across the back of the ballroom, illuminated by the setting sun? The towering plumes of headdresses nodding in the breeze of open terrace doors?

Chloe's first ball.

There had been unspoken drama over the ball, according to Aunt Caroline, for Viscountess Saddlerton always hosted the first spring ball. Only after invitations had been sent did Sir Jameson and Lady Severson announce the date of their ball — a full week before Lady Saddlerton's ball. Aunt Caroline had much to say on the matter throughout the week leading up to the Severson ball. According to her, this was nothing short of a declaration of a war between the two ladies. To Chloe's surprise, no one in or around Leongate would miss either ball if invited, so she could not understand the machinations at work but assumed it would all become clear as she became better acquainted with society and the social circles.

And so, the Severson ball had the pleasure of being Chloe's first. She had dressed with care, not only for the occasion but also to determine how she felt in her own skin, exposed for who she was rather than hidden behind a mask of rouge — or was that supposed to be enhanced by the blush of rouge?

With so much to see and so many familiar faces to greet, she had not a chance to search for Mr. Roberts or the Tindalls, although she tried. Time and again since the picnic, Mr. Roberts' words played in her head.

I like you, Miss Hudson.

I like who you are and the person I believe you will become....

... your greatest potential means becoming the best version of yourself....

Not long into the ball was she asked to dance by several gentlemen she had met at the previous parties. At this rate, she would promise every dance before Mr. Roberts or Mr. Tindall could ask her, assuming either intended to do so.

Mr. Roberts had been foremost on her mind. She wanted this evening to be an opportunity for them to share more about themselves. She *knew* she liked Mr. Roberts. Unequivocally. After his explanation of the slight during the soirée, there could be no question of her affection towards him.

Mr. Tindall had not escaped her thoughts so easily, however. She could not say in all honesty how she felt about him. He had never expressed intentions to court her, and was, for all intents and purposes, only the brother of her friend. His flirtations could have been the start of something. Was he the rogue her aunt seemed to think him, or were his flirtations genuine? Did it matter? She did not *like* Mr. Tindall, not as she liked Mr. Roberts, but there was something almost intoxicating about him, something that drew her to him.

They each deserved at least one dance. From there, she could better judge her feelings.

As the evening progressed, the sun dipping lower towards the horizon beyond those beckoning terrace doors, Chloe twirled, promenaded, and clicked her heels.

After her fourth dance, her breath short, perspiration trickling down her back, and a smile etched on her lips, she sashayed to the perimeter where Aunt Caroline was chatting with Mrs. Green and Mrs. Healy. Only moments did she have to exchange greetings before they were joined by none other than Mr. Roberts. Chloe stifled a squeak. The anticipation had built until her knees knocked at the sight of him.

"Miss Hudson," he said with a deep bow. "I hope you've saved a dance this evening for me."

Her fingers itched to touch her face, check if the sloppy-silly smile she felt on her lips was visible for all to see. He led her to the dancefloor and confirmed her memory had not deceived her to his dancing skill.

After the dance brought them together for the second time, he asked, "How is your mother enjoying the country air? I recall you mentioning her health brought you to the moors."

"She's loving it here. So much so, you and I may find ourselves Leongate neighbors for years to come. Papa has not yet begun a search for a more permanent residence. That, I'm to understand, is only because he loves the abbey and is reluctant to leave."

"Will we have the pleasure of their company at my aunt's ball next week?" He did not disguise the hope in his expression.

"I would like nothing less, but I think a ball might be too much for my mother, still. She did take a turn about the garden several times this week. Her strength is returning."

"If you've no objections, I will escort my aunt to call on them before the ball, ask after her health in person."

For the remainder of the dance, Chloe plotted ways to invite the family into the garden so that she might walk with Mr. Roberts.

As though reading her mind in part, he nodded to the terrace after the dance concluded. "A breath of fresh air, Miss Hudson, before your next admirer seeks a dance?"

Bowing her head to hide her flush of pleasure, she led the way to the terrace, the horizon an array of reds, the last vestiges of sunlight. A hand to the rail, she glanced inside to see her aunt talking with Lady Saddlerton — was the viscountess arranging to call on the Hudsons, or had that been a spontaneous offer by Mr. Roberts?

"Thank you, Mr. Roberts, for the dance," she said. "And thank you for what you said at the picnic. It's provided ample reflection."

He raised his brows, an almost eager grin her reply.

"I hope," she continued, "to drive to the ridge soon, test my boots against your moors. My aunt may fuss about the hike, but she's a secret lover of adventure."

A shadow blocked the doorway to the ballroom. Chloe and Mr. Roberts turned.

Mr. Tindall crossed to the railing in five strides to stand before Chloe. "I've found you at last, Miss Hudson. My sister has worried herself ill not knowing your whereabouts."

Chloe furrowed her brows, trying to get a better look inside the ballroom past Mr. Tindall. She had been at the ball for well over an hour but had not yet seen Miss Tindall, yet her friend had been searching for her?

"Come, Miss Hudson," he said, nodding back towards the ballroom. "I'll take you to her where you'll be safe from gentlemen who think little of your reputation."

Gasping at the rudeness to Mr. Roberts and to the reference of her reputation, she made to protest only to have Mr. Tindall talk over her, addressing Mr. Roberts this time.

"No chaperone on the terrace? You should know better, Mr. Roberts, especially after last time."

As Mr. Tindall cupped Chloe's elbow, Mr. Roberts stepped forward, as though to take the man to task.

Chloe took a step back and said, "I believe my aunt is waving to me. If you'll both excuse me." She dipped a slight curtsy, feeling wobbly and confused, then darted inside.

Aunt Caroline did not ask why Chloe chose to sit out the remaining dances, assuming, Chloe supposed, that her feet ached after the few she had enjoyed. In truth, Chloe wanted a moment to herself. It was only the one dance she was sitting out, technically, but to sit out one meant to sit out all to come. Not to dance was disappointing. But a moment to think took precedence.

What had occurred on the terrace? Something had occurred, however brief, however veiled. Mr. Tindall had tried to save her from compromise by Mr. Roberts. By her estimation, there had been no danger, as the terrace doors were open, and the terrace itself was in full view of the ballroom. There were other couples enjoying the sunset, as well, relishing the fresh air. And yet Mr. Tindall had implied there was a *last time*. What did he mean? Her aunt had seen Mr. Tindall as a rogue, but was Mr. Roberts the wolf in sheep's clothing? She could not believe it. She refused to believe it. What other sense did his comment make?

She need not have fretted for so long. Her questions were answered one dance later when Miss Tindall herself found Chloe and begged for an audience in private. Her friend seemed so distraught, Chloe assented, but not before telling Aunt Caroline she and Miss Tindall would be in the little parlor next to the refreshment room. Wary though her expression had been, Aunt Caroline nodded, adding a reminder that Chloe had promised to walk with her about the room at the end of this dance. Although Chloe had made no such promise, nor did she want to escape her friend's company, exactly, she felt an inexplicable relief to have a ready-made excuse.

"Oh, Miss Hudson," Miss Tindall began once they were seated, "I arrived late and began looking for you in earnest. You must believe how worried I was when I could not find you." She reached over to clasp Chloe's hands in hers. "When I saw you on the terrace with Mr. Roberts, I knew something had to be done. I sent my brother to rescue you. I'm so happy to see you safe."

Chloe squeezed her friend's hands. "Of course, I'm safe. Why would I not be? The terrace was in full view of the ballroom, and we only wished to take in the fresh air."

"You don't understand." Miss Tindall slipped her hands from Chloe's and retrieved a handkerchief. "What I say must not leave this room. Can you keep this secret?"

"Rest assured."

"It's Mr. Roberts. He's not what he seems. You must see how close my brother and I are. He's protective of me, more so now than ever. All because of Mr. Roberts. I thought to protect you by guiding you away from him, but I see now it'll take more than good will. You must know the truth." She held the handkerchief to her lips, as though to stifle a sob. "It was at my neighbor's Christmas party. I had grown tired of the merriment and sought refuge in the library. I planned only to be there a few moments in which to compose myself — a touch too much wine, you understand — but when I tried to leave, Mr. Roberts entered, blocking the door. I made light of it, hoping to slip past, but he came with ill intent. I tell you, Miss Hudson, I never led him to believe I would welcome his advances. He paid me compliments, then he demanded I reciprocate with a… a… a kiss."

Chloe covered her mouth with her hand, appalled and shocked beyond words.

"My brother entered the library at that very moment, worried for my health, only to find Mr. Roberts' hands on my arms as he tried to force his kiss. I thought it would all end in a duel. I was so afraid for my brother. He ensured my safety by ushering me from the room. I know not what was discussed between them, only that Mr. Roberts never bothered me again. But, Miss Hudson, he almost ruined my reputation. What if it had been someone other than my brother to come into the room?"

Of all the things to fear, Chloe's thoughts were not on the reputation. And yet, that was certainly a warranted fear. So caught up in Miss Hudson's tale of horror, Chloe had forgotten they were talking about Mr. Roberts.

Mr. Roberts?

Surely not.

Chloe's mind reeled, the man she knew at odds with the man Miss Tindall described. Then, what did Chloe know of him or the behaviors of rogues? How had Aunt Caroline not seen through the sheep's clothing? She could spot a rogue in a crowd, yet nothing gave her pause about Mr. Roberts, seeing instead Mr. Tindall as the potential villain. Miss Tindall's experience, however, could not be ignored.

The parlor door opened, sending Miss Tindall jumping to her feet in fright and Chloe furrowing her brows. Mr. Tindall stepped into the room, his expression that of a concerned brother.

Miss Tindall shot forward, wrapping her arms around her brother's neck. "I've told her, Jeffrey. I've confessed what happened."

He patted her on the back, looking at Chloe from over his sister's shoulder. "Allow me to fetch you both a drink."

"No, don't leave," Miss Tindall said with a hic-cupped sob. "Stay and assure Miss Hudson we'll look after her. You know how worried I was when I saw her alone with Mr. Roberts. I'll collect drinks for us. I need a moment to steady my nerves."

Chloe stood, her gaze moving from Mr. Tindall to Miss Tindall, her thoughts on the next moments to come — Miss Tindall was to bring drinks, leaving her and Mr. Tindall alone in the parlor? That did not make sense. In light of what Miss Tindall had divulged, it sounded part hypocritical to leave Chloe in the room alone with a gentleman but also part reassuring, for Mr. Tindall had been the protector of innocence and was even now playing that role. No harm could come. Besides, they were next door to the refreshments. And yet, Chloe's hands felt clammy in her gloves.

Miss Tindall made for the door.

Mr. Tindall crossed the room to join Chloe.

Chloe blinked, indecisive.

It might have ended like this...

"Miss Tindall," Chloe cried out. "Wait. I'll attend you. You're upset, and I would not wish you to be alone."

The excuse to leave the room sounded reasonable enough, not as though she was avoiding being alone with Mr. Tindall.

Mr. Tindall said, "My sister wishes for a moment alone to compose herself." He held out his hands. "Come to me. Allow me to reassure you of your safety from blackguards like Mr. Roberts."

Chloe stepped towards Miss Tindall, who stood with her hand on the door handle. "If you'll both excuse me, then, I would like to see to my aunt. I had promised to take a turn about the room with her and fear I have stayed overlong."

Panic began to swell in her breast. With so much to consider, she could not say what frightened her, being alone with Mr. Tindall, being caught alone with Mr. Tindall, or the villainy that had been divulged about Mr. Roberts. All these things. As Miss Tindall claimed for herself, Chloe, too, needed a moment to compose herself, to collect her thoughts and sift through the information.

"Miss Hudson," Miss Tindall said in a huff. "I won't be but two seconds. Has it not occurred to you that my brother wishes to speak to you in private for those two seconds? Allow him that courtesy after all he's done for me."

Chloe turned to Mr. Tindall's expectant gaze, his hands still outstretched, then back to Miss Tindall, whose expression bore one of annoyance to be delayed in departure more than a wish to recover from her recent upset. It was that expression more than anything that moved Chloe towards the door rather than towards Mr. Tindall.

At that moment, the parlor door swung open, nudging Miss Tindall none too gently.

Standing in the doorway, Mr. Roberts surveyed the room, his eyes alighting on Chloe before spying the Tindalls, his brows working as though trying to decipher if he was interrupting, his presence nefarious or well timed.

Heart in her throat, she struggled with conflicting feelings, relief of Mr. Roberts' intrusion and concern about his behavior with Miss Tindall. Rather than wait for someone else to decide her fate, she accepted his presence as divine intervention. However well intended might be the Tindalls, Chloe could not deny her discomfort.

"Mr. Roberts," Chloe said on an exhale. "My aunt has sent you to fetch me? I thought she might be feeling anxious at my tardiness."

Without blinking an eye, Mr. Roberts said, "You are correct, Miss Hudson. Mrs. Riley was caught in conversation by Lady Saddlerton or she would have come herself. Shall I take you to her now?"

The tension in the air was palpable, gooseflesh shivering across Chloe's skin. A glance to Miss Tindall revealed a face of outrage. A glance to Mr. Tindall was no less friendly, the latter taking a step towards Mr. Roberts. It ought to have been a casual moment, one in which friends were chatting in a parlor only to be interrupted by a needy aunt desiring a companion, but that did not seem the case to Chloe. Something had shifted.

Something that could not shift back. Not if pressed could Chloe explain the sensation. In a peculiar way, it seemed by going with Mr. Roberts that she had made a choice, a choice with whom she sided, which was perfectly ridiculous, for that was like choosing between the lion and the tiger when Mr. Roberts had just been revealed as a rogue, yet Mr. Tindall made her nervous.

Knowing this was a decision from which she could not turn back, she made the choice by faith, by instinct, by trust. After all, despite her aunt's choices in life, Aunt Caroline had never been mistaken.

Chloe crossed the room to stand beside Mr. Roberts.

With a final pivot into the room, she said, "Thank you both for your advice and friendship."

Nary a word was said as Mr. Roberts closed the parlor door behind them and escorted Chloe past the refreshments.

Only when he reached for the door leading to the ballroom did he pause. "A lemonade, Miss Hudson? You look… faint."

"No, but thank you. I—I wish to return to the terrace with you, if you wouldn't object."

He raised his eyebrows, not disguising his surprise. While they both knew he had not been sent by her aunt, Chloe suspected he anticipated that was to whom she expected him to take her.

"Lead the way, Miss Hudson."

She did. As they circled the perimeter of the room, Chloe caught her aunt's eye, unspoken words exchanged.

The terrace was bathed in early moonlight this time. It was not dimly lit, however. Flickering flames ensconced in rainbow-colored lanterns adorned the eaves of the house, supplying ample light for the other guests enjoying the evening air. All around them, couples and groups talked, some watching the dancers inside, otherwise gazing at the moonrise.

Mr. Roberts spoke first. "Am I a villain or hero for interrupting? When I saw you both retreat to the parlor, and then Mr. Tindall follow, I... worried. Was that foolish of me? She is your friend, after all."

"The more fool I, Mr. Roberts. Friends should not cause each other discomfort, however well intentioned." Chloe clasped the terrace railing, hoping to imbue herself with strength. "I understand you and Miss Tindall once courted."

Next to her, Mr. Roberts sucked in a sharp breath. "No, we did not, although I'm surprised she would have called it courting. Before I say what I'm about to say, is your friendship with the Tindalls at an end or intact?"

Regardless what Mr. Roberts said, she knew the friendship ended when she stepped out of the parlor. Just as she had said to him, no friend should cause discomfort, and that was what she had suffered with each encounter of the Tindalls. Perhaps it was not their fault. Perhaps it was nothing more than a difference in personality.

Chloe could ignore her intuition no longer. "It is at an end," she assured Mr. Roberts.

When he did not immediately respond, she thought he had not heard her. She angled to see him better, one side of his face tinged blue from the colored lanterns.

At length, he said, "The Tindalls and I move in different social circles, but one cannot escape the acquaintance in so small a place as Leongate. I've known of them and their family for years, ever since they moved here, but they spend more time in London. Prior to this Christmas, I had little dealings with them aside from the knowing *of* them. As I have little doubt that my aunt apprised you of my familial wealth, you must be aware not all families are well meaning. The Tindalls are known gamblers, sometimes successful and other times stretched thin. Ah, I'm talking in circles, aren't I, rambling my way to answer your unasked question."

"No, I'm following you. Please continue."

Whatever he was leading to, it could be a lie. He had been accused of taking advantage of Miss Tindall, after all, so why would he not lie? How could Chloe believe anything he said?

Her aunt did not make mistakes.

Her faith did not lie.

Her intuition squeezed her heart to *listen* and *trust*.

Mr. Roberts continued, "At a Christmas party, I was invited to the library by Mr. Tindall, presumably to admire a collection of his neighbor's classic texts. If you had seen my own library at this juncture in the conversation, you would understand why this would interest me enough not to question the invitation. When I arrived at the library, it was to find Miss Tindall instead. Alone. We were not together for more than a minute. It was planned. She embraced me just as her brother opened the door. It was so obviously planned, I felt sick to my core and did not know how to extricate myself."

He paused, but it was clear by his mannerism that he was not finished. Chloe would not have known how to respond even if he were. What he described was so unlikely, yet she could perfectly envision the Tindalls behaving in just such a manner. Had this been their plan during the parlor? A reverse of Miss Tindall or someone else catching Chloe with Mr. Tindall? Surely not. And yet...

"What I've never understood," Mr. Roberts continued, "was why they were not after a marriage proposal, rather money. You see, if it had not been so theatrical, I would have been obligated as a gentleman to offer for her, regardless of the whole event being a mistake of wrong time and wrong place. But it was theatrical, dramatic, Mr. Tindall himself offering the out. He would demand satisfaction unless I paid him for his silence. I had thought myself compromised. I had thought them in expectation of my proposal. I would have offered for her, you know, for I am nothing if not an honorable gentleman. But it was all about money."

"You *paid* them?" So shocked, Chloe could not keep from asking.

Mr. Roberts nodded. "They've not bothered me since. Not until now, until I expressed an interest in you. You'll forgive me for not explaining this sooner. You understand why I did not, yes?"

"I do. I'm glad you've divulged now, even when you must be hesitant to share, fearing what I might make of the situation and you along with it. I trust what you've said, and I trust you."

He inched his hand until their fingertips touched on the railing. "Then, if I may be so bold, I would like nothing more than to invite you and your aunt for that once-promised drive to Blakey Ridge. Is next week too soon?"

Tugging her bottom lip between her teeth and thankful her blush would not be visible, not between the moonlight on one side and the cascade of lantern color on the other, Chloe said, "Tomorrow would not be too soon, Mr. Roberts."

"William. My Christian name is William."

"Call me Chloe," she said, before lacing her fingers with his and tugging him towards the ballroom, eager to share their alliance with Aunt Caroline.

Or it could have ended like this...

Studying Mr. Tindall's expression, his open concern, his honest regard, Chloe chose to trust him, trust Miss Tindall, to trust her faith in friendship.

She nodded to her friend. "Lemonade, please. Nothing stronger."

The parlor door closed behind Miss Tindall.

In five strides, Mr. Tindall crossed the room to Chloe, clasping her upper arms. His grasp, both strong and protective, had Chloe trembling in his embrace. Was this what she wanted? Perspiration pooled along her spine — fear or anticipation? A combination of both. A heady combination. Why had she never felt this with any of the encounters with Mr. Roberts? Her intuition had warned her, then, that Mr. Roberts was not the right choice, a rogue in sheep's clothing.

Mr. Tindall had always been forthright, intentions never veiled.

"You're safe, Miss Hudson," he said, his hands hot and tight about her sleeves, his breath brandy-touched, intoxicating, warming her cheeks with each word. "We'll ensure Mr. Roberts does not molest you. So much as a glance from him, and he'll have me to answer to. You accept my protection?"

Chloe stuttered, uncertain how to respond. Was it only protection he offered, as a brother offers for a sister? A friend for another friend? She had thought he wanted more. She had worn rouge to the soirée in the hope he had wanted more. Her aunt's tale of woe played in her ears. Her aunt could not have regretted her choices, making the same choice twice, as she did. Both husbands had lived fast lives that brought them to an untimely demise, but they were lives full of adventure and passion. Chloe wanted it all. Mr. Tindall's friends had bored her. His card games had bored her. But *he* did not bore her. He dizzied her mind until she could think of nothing except him.

"I offer you my protection, Miss Hudson. Please accept."

"I don't know what that means," Chloe managed, her voice hoarse, her words little more than a whisper.

"It means I care for you, perhaps more than you understand. I see in you a remarkable woman who ought to be by my side, not only for my protection but for my affection. With my guidance, with my love, I shall see you in full bloom, a woman of stunning maturity, the most admired of all society beauties. Allow me, Miss Hudson, *Chloe*, to love you as you ought to be loved. Allow me to help you reach your potential."

He dipped his head, his gaze on her lips.

Chloe's breath sharpened, smothered by his masculinity, his promises, his everything. Her hands to his chest, she closed her eyes, desperate for him to fulfill those promises before his sister returned.

The parlor door opened.

Rather than Miss Tindall with drinks, Mr. Roberts stood in the doorway, looking from Chloe to Mr. Tindall. "A remarkable semblance to *last time*, is it not, Mr. Tindall? Staged for my benefit, or am I truly to wish you both happy?"

Chloe stepped away from Mr. Tindall and parted her lips to reply, but then what could she say? He had not offered marriage. He had offered her only protection, protection against this same man, no less, the true villain who had accosted Miss Tindall. How curious it was that Mr. Roberts turned out to be the rogue. His face, one of anger, revealed all. He had been duped, his villainy exposed.

Mr. Tindall slipped an arm in front of Chloe as he took one step to block her from Mr. Roberts. "I believe you've lost your way, sir. There is nothing here for you."

Mr. Roberts eyed Chloe, as though waiting for a protest, a plea for help, something. At length, he said, "My mistake."

"Let it be your last. This woman is under my protection from this moment forward."

As Mr. Roberts bowed out of the room, Miss Tindall sidestepped past him. So distracted by seeing Mr. Roberts storm to the parlor door, she must have forgotten to grab the drinks, for she had arrived empty handed.

Before Chloe could remark on the beverages or Miss Tindall to offer a comment, Mr. Tindall turned to face Chloe, wrapping an arm around her shoulders, a possessive, protective arm, one that made Chloe feel more than dizzy this time. She felt claimed.

"I believe," Mr. Tindall said, "we should finish what we started before we were interrupted." With his free hand, he traced the curve of Chloe's face. "I will ensure you never regret your choice, my rosebud."

As he lowered to meet her lips at last, she relaxed into his arms, knowing her aunt would understand the alliance of her choice, an alliance of the heart.

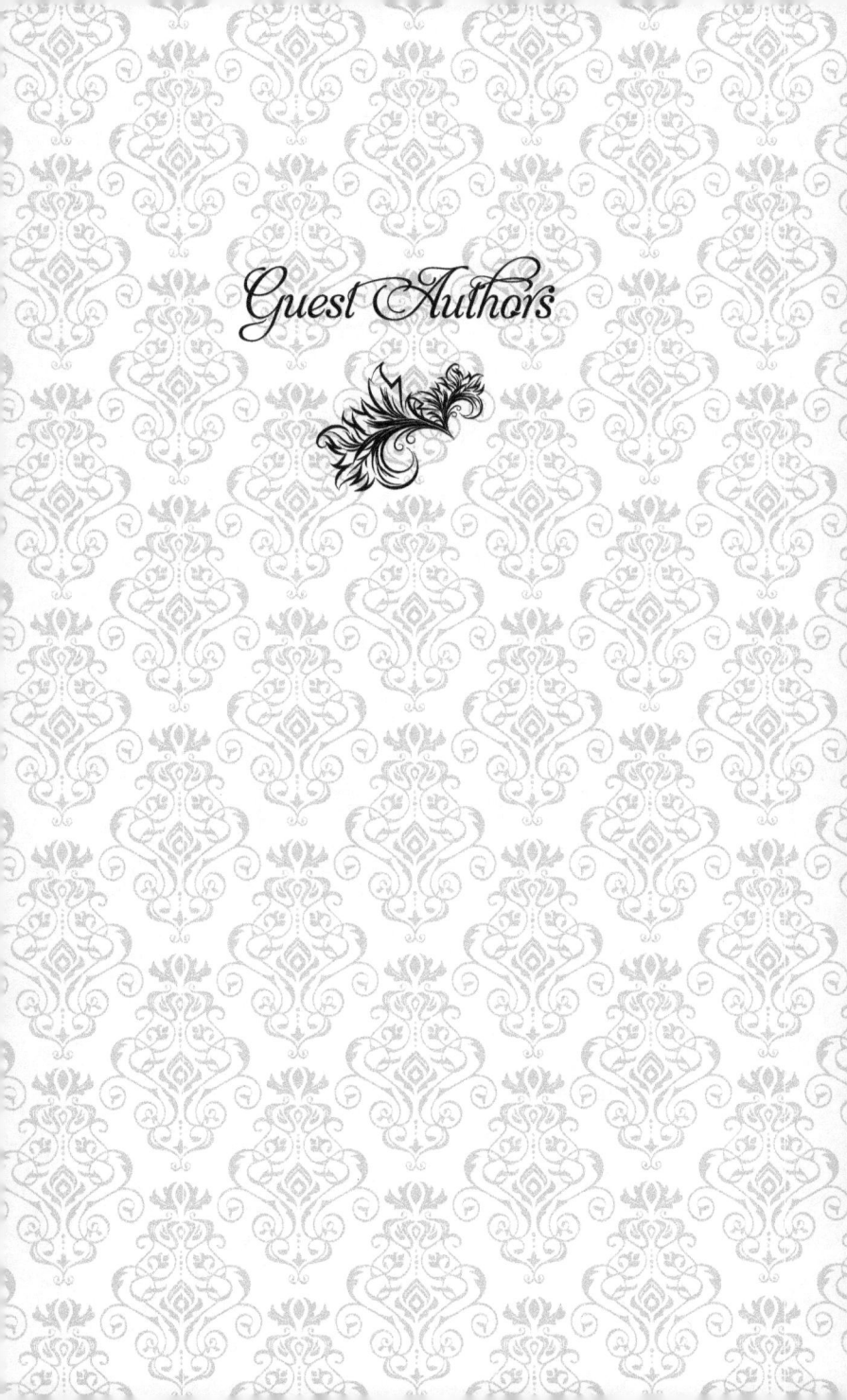

Guest Authors

We Happy Few

By Abbie Grubb

Elizabeth squared her shoulders. Tonight was the night. She trailed up the stairs behind her aunt and entered the ballroom. She gazed longingly at the far seats along the wall where she had so often taken refuge with the other wallflowers. Even they were likely to shun her tonight. Perhaps if she hadn't been so desperate for a friend, she would not have been caught with him alone. She shook her head to dispel the thought and focused on surviving her first appearance in society since her scandal two weeks earlier.

Her aunt glared at her over her shoulder as if daring her to step out of line again. Ignoring the look, she moved away from her aunt's condemnation, holding her head high as she moved further into the room. She smoothed her gown and checked her reflection in a window as she passed. Despite being rather pale, she was pleased with her overall appearance this evening and hoped it would give her confidence to face the lions. Her long straight hair was arranged in a simple but stylish coiffure and her cream-colored gown embellished with small rosebuds on the skirt and trim swirled around her as she circled the ballroom.

A gathering of older women her aunt's age cast dark glances at Elizabeth as she walked past. She wondered to herself whether such women practiced their pursed lips since they were so efficient at the gesture. She moved on ignoring the glares and whispers. Years of being on the outskirts of high society had prepared her to face the consequences of her scandal. And yet, she was fast realizing that she would prefer her former invisibility to open hostility.

She skirted the edge of the crowd, scanning the room for the Duke of Waverly. Jack. Despite his request over tea the day before, she could not imagine calling His Grace, Jack. Waverly had been nothing but kind to her since the incident, but part of her wondered if that did not make it worse. Neglect she was used to. Kindness and understanding was new territory for her.

In the two weeks since the scandal he had called on her nearly every day, walking with her through the gardens or taking tea in the drawing room. Despite the strained circumstances of their first meeting, she had come to look forward to his visits. When Aunt Margaret was present she often made it uncomfortable with thinly veiled critiques of "Silly Eliza," and her situation, but he had handled the unpleasantness with grace and a quick change of topic each time.

As she neared the refreshment table, she heard rather than saw the familiar trio of young women approaching from her left. She looked around for anything she might use as a distraction. Turning to the right, she reached for a glass of lemonade, keeping her back to the room and examining the table scape with great concentration as the group giggled their way past her.

"Shocking behavior..." Elizabeth heard one of the girls say in a loud whisper.

"I would be too ashamed to show my face..." crowed another as they moved past.

She sighed, set her empty cup on the table, and stared at the wall intently. She would far rather admire the candles in their wall sconces than give the three ladies the satisfaction of cutting her direct if she turned around.

She moved further to her right in the opposite direction of Miss Sophia Carter and her two shadows, Miss Annabelle Simpson and Miss Catherine Stone. If she had known they would never welcome an orphaned relation into their circle, she could have saved herself from scandal. She should have known.

Once the three young ladies had moved past her, Elizabeth turned to better watch the couples as they lined up for a reel, smiling and laughing at their partners and friends across the lines of dancers. She loved dancing and had never been a wallflower by choice. It wasn't that she didn't want to be a part of the pack, but rather that she had never found *her* pack.

She sighed and debated whether it was too soon to return to the refreshment table. It was obvious now that coming tonight had been a mistake. No friendly smiles met her gaze as she scanned the room. No gentlemen approached her to partner in the dances. Not even her wallflower companions from balls past would acknowledge her. She was tarnished in the eyes of society.

Her longing for friendship had paved the way to her own ruin and she knew she had no one to blame but herself. It was all so obvious in retrospect.

Miss Carter and her friends had greeted her almost as soon as she had arrived at the Dowager Duchess of Waverly's dinner party two weeks ago. Even that should have aroused her suspicion, but loneliness had prevailed over reason. When the ladies retired to the drawing room after dinner, the young women had fallen into a quiet discussion of the finer qualities of the man of the house, the Duke of Waverly.

Sophia arched a brow and looked at Elizabeth as she spoke, "I heard that Waverly has returned from England to claim his inheritance and is ready to take a wife," whispered Sophia. "I am quite sure we would make a fine match, would we not?" she queried, quite unconcerned with a response.

Annabelle leaned in excitedly. "I heard from his sister, Jane, that His Grace keeps a diary of sorts in the library. He writes his calendar and personal thoughts in a small book."

"Oh, what I would not give to know his passions and dislikes," exclaimed Sophia. "I wonder if he has written of me when we shared a dance?" She looked down her nose at Elizabeth and added, "we danced twice at the Montgomery's ball last week."

"According to Jane, he is gone on estate business at present." Annabelle said in a loud whisper "He never appeared at dinner, so I am sure he is not at home or he would certainly attend his mother's party."

Catherine simpered, "I would retrieve the book from the library for you, Sophia, but I am not nearly courageous enough."

Annabelle's eyes widened and she echoed her friend. "My nerves shake at the mere thought of such a thing."

Sophia laid a reassuring hand on her friend's arms. "I would never ask either of you to do such a thing."

Three pairs of eyes had looked towards Elizabeth. The gauntlet was thrown down. Sophia voiced the challenge. "You are so much more brave than we are, Eliza. And you are at home in a library and are often quiet. Won't you fetch the book so that we might all learn more about Waverly?" Now she reached her hand out and rested it on Elizabeth's hand. "Would you do that for your friends?"

Elizabeth stared at the hand resting on hers, as her fear and excitement battled. "I wouldn't even know where to go," she began, but she paused at the looks of anger and disappointment she saw. Looking between Sophia, Catherine, and Annabelle, she swallowed her concerns and met Sophia's eyes. "Can you tell me how to get to the library?"

With the promise of friendship dangled before her, Elizabeth agreed to retrieve the book without truly thinking about what she was doing. In her nervousness, she forgot her candle until she was moving through the dark hallways of the Duke's home. She came to the door of the library and pushed it open a touch. A faint light glowed from the fireplace as she moved into the room, and she was just able to see the back of a large settee in front of the hearth.

According to Annabelle, Waverly hid his notes under the settee. She crept up to the back of the furniture and moved around the foot of the piece. Glancing behind her to the door once more, she dropped to her hands and knees and began crawling along its length and feeling for the book underneath. With head down and heart racing, she clawed at the floor below the settee for what felt like hours before coming up empty.

In a moment of despair over letting down her 'friends,' she slumped forward against the settee, knocking into it far harder than she had intended. The furniture shifted across the floor startling a very-present dozing Waverly from a peaceful sleep on said settee. She later learned that Annabelle was only partially right. He *had* traveled for the estate that day but had returned tired and dirty and had chosen to forego the dinner, relaxing instead in his favorite room of the manor.

Waverly had sat up, startled awake by the movement and startled further by the closeness of a pale face in the firelight. Eliza had known immediately who he was, but the same could not be said of him. Without thinking, he had reached for her, grabbing her by the shoulders as he sat up, pulling her up off the floor. He blinked and shook his head as if trying to dispel a dream, or perhaps a nightmare. Elizabeth could do nothing, but simply stared at him in surprise.

"Who are you," he said softly. He glanced at the floor beside her and his brow furrowed. "Why were you on the floor?"

He slid his hands down her arms as if to warm or calm her, but still she made no response, only stared at him wide eyed. "What is your name?" he asked again.

This time, she had managed to croak out, "Elizabeth."

He moved to sit up, keeping his hands on her arms. "Well, Elizabeth, why were you on the floor of my family library? Are you unwell?"

A noise sounded behind him and they both froze. In an instant, the reality of their situation hit them both. Alone, in a darkened room, in what could only be described as an intimate embrace. Elizabeth's face paled and if possible, her eyes grew wider. Waverly's eyes closed briefly as if in resignation.

The door to the library flung open. The Dowager Duchess of Waverly, his mother, stood illuminated by a large candle glancing about the room and muttering something about 'privacy' and 'thieves.' Sophia, Annabelle, and Catherine crowded into the doorway behind her looking properly aghast at the situation as it unfolded.

Waverly lightly squeezed Elizabeth's arms, before releasing her. He stood and reached down to help her from her kneeling position. She took the hand he offered, but moved away once she stood. She could not meet his eyes.

Despite Elizabeth's protestations to her innocence, her insistence that she had not even known he was there, and the fact that they hardly knew one another after his years of absence at school and abroad, the damage was done.

Shaking her head to dispel the images from the fateful dinner party, Elizabeth looked around the crowded room for an escape. She moved towards the large doors at the rear of the ballroom that opened onto the terrace and gardens. She pushed open the doors with more force than was probably necessary, angry at herself for falling prey to their manipulation. "Were you so desperate?" she wondered aloud into the cool evening air.

"Who leaves a diary under a settee anyway?" She pondered in her quiet personal tirade as she moved further away from the grand house and closer to the walkways and hedges of the formal gardens. Two men moved out of the house not too far behind her, and she attempted to angle away from them, lest she be characterized as both scandalous *and* mentally unstable.

Elizabeth paused in her walk through the gardens, wrapping her arms across her waist and leaning against a small arched gate among the rows of hedges. She could still remember everything so clearly. The warmth of his touch on her shoulders and the kindness he had shown her that night, despite the awkwardness of the situation. In the weeks since, he had even begun to tease her about that night. In the privacy of the gardens she closed her eyes and allowed herself a small smile at the thought of him.

Her eyes flew open. Three familiar high-pitched voices approaching from behind brought her out of her reverie. She tensed, unsure whether to try to move into the gardens and avoid a confrontation or face them head on. Before she could decide, Sophia was in front of her, arms folded across her stylish gown and a smirk contorting her pretty pale features. Elizabeth sensed Annabelle and Catherine move around behind her. She felt like a trapped animal facing a predator, but was unsure of how to respond to the threat.

Sophia tossed her blond curls in annoyance. "You can't do anything right, can you? You were supposed to help me win Waverly with the diary, but you went and got caught with him yourself." She smirked at Elizabeth. "Not that it will do you any good. *I* would have at least emerged with an engagement if I were foolish enough to be caught."

Annabelle and Catherine laughed, but Elizabeth bristled.

"Foolish?" Elizabeth retorted. "The only foolish thing I did was try to be your friend." Eliza crossed her arms. "I think you wanted me to be caught!"

Sophia threw her hands in the air in a most un-ladylike manner. "Why would I want such a thing? The intention was for *me* to marry him, not you! How were you stupid enough not to see a man on the couch!? Besides, what else was I supposed to say when his mother asked where you were?"

Elizabeth balled her hands into fists at her sides, her eyes burning and a lump rising in her throat. She glared at Sophia.

Annabelle and Catherine moved in closer behind Elizabeth. What were they planning to do to her? How far would they take their frustrations?

Heavy footsteps approached from the house. All four women peered through the soft light of the garden to see who drew closer. Elizabeth debated who it might be and whether they would be an improvement. Given the direction the evening had taken, she was inclined to think things could only get worse.

From behind Sophia appeared the two men that Eliza had seen at the garden doors. Her shoulders relaxed as she recognized them. One was a full head taller than the other, but they had similarly brown hair, green eyes, and high cheekbones that implied they were related. As they neared, the taller one spoke.

"Ah, Miss Elizabeth, there you are!" The taller of the gentleman reached for her hand and bowed low over it in greeting. "We have been looking all over for you. It is so good to see you."

For her part, Eliza nearly had to pick her jaw up from the garden floor, so surprised was she by this familiar greeting. Two of Waverly's best friends were obviously playing a game of their own by coming to her rescue. By sheer force of habit, she gave him her hand and curtsied, but it was a full ten seconds before she regained her ability to speak.

"It is a pleasure to see you as well...Lord Raven-wood, Lord Radcliff." Eliza had never been formally introduced to either man, but every eligible young lady of London knew who they were. The taller was the Earl of Ravenwood and the shorter was his cousin the Earl of Radcliff. Along with Waverly and Captain Edward Kilpatrick, recently returned from his Majesty's service on the continent, they were best friends and the most talked about men of the season.

Radcliff stepped forward and reached for Eliza's arm. He tucked it neatly into his. He pulled her from her shocked state and began moving back towards the house speaking pleasantries about the weather and garden statuaries the whole way. From the corner of her eye, she saw Ravenwood give a tight aristocratic nod to Sophia, Annabelle, and Catherine before falling in step behind the two of them.

The Earl steered Elizabeth out of the gardens and back towards the terrace where light and music spilled out into the warm evening. He slowed his pace and looked down at Eliza's countenance, his chatter ceasing.

"Please forgive our manners, Miss Elizabeth, but Waverly was worried about your last experience with society and asked us to keep an eye on you this evening.

Elizabeth flushed at the reference and stopped walking. She turned and looked up at him. "I cannot thank you enough for your bad manners, Lord Radcliff," she said through a tentative smile, her first of the evening. "Will His Grace be attending the ball?" She asked, with only a slight tremor in her voice.

"He would not miss it for the world, Miss Elizabeth," Lord Ravenwood assured her.

A look passed between the two men as if they shared a joke, but she did not press for an explanation.

Radcliff extended his arm to her again. "Shall we return to the ballroom? I for one would like nothing more than to partner you for the next dance."

As Radcliff escorted her into place for the next dance, he whispered, "Waverly warned us that we could only dance once with you, and I would not want to miss my opportunity." With a wink he placed her hand in his and they were off, leaving her little time to ponder his statement.

Despite the strain of the evening, she could not help but enjoy the dancing, first with Radcliff then with Ravenwood. Both men complimented her gown, praised her dancing abilities, and kept her laughing throughout the two sets with stories of their days at Eton. When they left the dance floor, the two gentlemen guided her across the crowded space to the refreshment table, offering her a lemonade.

As she lifted her second cup of the evening to her lips, she breathed deeply and reveled in the change she felt. The sideways glances and murmurs had not disappeared, but they seemed more confused than condemning. The support of two earls, no matter how brief or unexpected, could not be ignored.

As she gazed around the room, watching the dancing couples spin and move in time with the musicians in the gallery, she continued to look for Waverly. As nervous as she was to see him here, it would be best to get their first public meeting out of the way.

She moved around the room with Radcliff and more than once she caught herself holding her breath at the sight of a tall figure with dark curls, but each time she was disappointed. She remained close to either Radcliff or Ravenwood and was relieved to be greeted politely by all she encountered while by their sides.

As she listened to Radcliff joke with another gentleman, she scanned the room again for Waverly, but instead her eyes landed on his sister.

Jane approached from across the room, a sweet smile on her face. Unsure of what to expect, Eliza tensed but kept a smile plastered on her face as she approached.

His sister was all light to her brother's darkness. She had long blonde tresses, swept up into a becoming arrangement woven with ribbons and roses of soft pink. She reached out for Elizabeth's hands, and her smile was so sincere Eliza could not help but relax. She dipped in greeting to the younger woman and took her hands, happy to receive a warm welcome.

"Miss Elizabeth, you look stunning this evening," exclaimed Jane, relieving her from the strain of what to say first.

"I could say the same to you," Eliza replied, admiring the young woman's fashionable gown of pink with lace at the bodice and sleeves.

Taking a step back to look at her, Jane gushed, "Jack will be speechless when he arrives." She leaned in and continued at a conspiratorial volume, "He will deny it if you ask, but he is as nervous as a sinner in church about this evening. He nearly drove us all mad with questions about his tailcoat options." She turned to stand next to Elizabeth and looped her arm through hers as if they had been friends all their lives.

Elizabeth flushed as she sorted through this new information. Why would Jack – His Grace – be nervous? As quickly as she had flushed, she paled. Perhaps he was embarrassed and nervous about what censure he might face in her company.

She looked at the floor, blinking back the tears that had threatened so often lately.

She felt Jane's arm stiffen and looked up to see the cause of her discomfiture.

Walking towards them was a handsome yet unsmiling young man in uniform. His posture, red hair, and clothes were immaculate approaching the perfection one might see in a fashion plate save for a black eye patch over his left eye. He executed a perfect bow to Jane, then turned a curious gaze to Elizabeth.

"Eliza, I don't believe you have met the captain yet. Elizabeth, this is Captain Kilpatrick. Captain, this is Miss Elizabeth Stanton." Elizabeth curtsied as the soldier bowed in return.

"Lady Jane, Miss Elizabeth," he intoned, his voice soft and deep. His gaze seemed to linger on Jane

before he pulled it to Eliza. "May I have the pleasure of this next dance, Miss Elizabeth?"

"It would be my honor Captain Kilpatrick," she
replied placing her hand in his to be led to the floor.

Eliza did not know when this dream would end,
but she had decided to enjoy it while she could. Her
dance with the captain was not so frivolous as her
first two of the evening had been, but Kilpatrick spoke
softly to her when they were close enough to converse,
telling her how he had met Waverly and the others
while they were at school together.

"We bonded over a shared homesickness and dis-
dain for our headmaster. All of us left as soon as we
could, but I am forever grateful for my time at Eton.
I cannot imagine coming of age without my 'Band
of Brothers.'"

"Henry V, from Shakespeare," Elizabeth exclaimed,
recognizing the reference. "There are other works I
prefer to the Bard's plays, but what a lovely sentiment.
It must be wonderful to have such close friends," she
said wistfully.

He smiled down at her as they spun through the
motions. "Waverly said you would know the reference." She felt her face flush as they continued to
dance but even she could not distinguish whether it
was from embarrassment at her bookishness or pleasure at the compliment.

The music drew to a close and Elizabeth was
again left with little time to consider all she had heard
about Waverly before the Captain escorted her back
to where Jane stood with Radcliff and Ravenwood.

She had barely caught her breath when she heard
a high-pitched voice from behind her.

"I cannot understand your choice of companions tonight, Lady Jane. Two rakes, a blind pensioner, and a scandalous orphan seem far beneath you."

Elizabeth gasped at the audacity of such an insult.

She turned to face Miss Carter and felt both shock and pity at the sight of her. Sophia's normally calm, pale, and proper demeanor was replaced by a red-faced, angry visage that more resembled a hissing cat than a young woman. Annabelle and Catherine stood behind her, scowling at the assemblage.

Above the din, a clear baritone voice rang out, "I am confident that I misheard you Miss Carter." The ballroom fell silent at the bold voice of the Duke of Waverly. "Surely you did not just insult my sister, my best friends, and my betrothed, did you?"

Eliza's breath caught in her throat and her heart skipped a beat at the sound.

Betrothed?

Before she could make sense of the word, she felt a hand rest lightly on the small of her back and a solid, warm presence filled the space beside her. Still holding her breath, she looked up, meeting the kind brown eyes that looked back at her.

Jane stood to the other side of Waverly, her arm resting on the sleeve of Captain Kilpatrick. Ravenwood and Radcliff moved to stand next to Eliza, buoying her fragile spirits in an otherwise tempestuous evening..

Elizabeth cocked her eyebrows at Sophia as if echoing Waverly's question. Annabelle and Catherine tugged on her arms to pull her away.

Shrinking under the gaze of her six antagonists, Sophia managed a slight curtsy and choked out, "No, Your Grace," before disappearing into the crowd.

At her departure, the room seemed to take a collective breath as the next set began and the gathered assembly turned to one another to discuss the evening's excitement.

Jane moved in front of Elizabeth, taking her hand and squeezing it as she placed a light kiss on her cheek. "I will be so happy to have a sister," she whispered. With another squeeze of her hand, she left, partnering with the Captain for a dance.

Ravenwood turned to her bowing low over her hand. "It was a pleasure to meet you, Miss Elizabeth. Welcome to the family." With a wink from Radcliff, the two of them moved away leaving her with Waverly.

She turned to face him, warmth flooding her as she looked up at him wanting to say so much but unsure where to start. They may as well have been the only two in the room, though hundreds of prying eyes and ears surrounded them pretending to ignore them. He raised his hand as if to touch her face, then seemed to think better of it and instead took her hand.

"Miss Stanton, please forgive me for keeping you in the dark." He wrapped both hands around hers and held them tightly. "I knew from the moment I awoke with my arms around you that I would offer for you, but I did not want you to be forced into something you did not want. I wanted you to get to know me. I wanted to know more about you too. And I wanted to make sure it was me and not my diary you really wanted."

Eliza smiled through her tears and his face brightened at her response.

He reached up and pushed a curl away from her face. "You have a curl that always escapes your ribbons and now that I'm standing so close to you, I see you have three freckles on your nose." His smile broadened. "During the last two weeks, you asked about my family, expressed your sorrow at the loss of my father, and learned how much sugar I take in my tea by my second visit. I learned that you look lovely in pink and for some reason you prefer reading to archery."

Elizabeth laughed at his accurate statement. "You would too if you were as bad of a shot as I am," she explained.

He smiled and squeezed her hand. "We do not know each other well yet, but what I know I have come to love. I choose to believe that love will only grow as we learn more. You braved society alone tonight while I visited your uncle to settle our terms, but I never want you to feel alone again, Eliza. I hope it was not too presumptuous on my part to assume you would do me the honor of becoming my wife?"

"It was not too presumptuous, Your Grace," Elizabeth said, her vision blurring.

"Jack," he whispered, touching his forehead to hers and pulling her close.

A Minor Deception

By H.J. Palmer

"He only met our Sophie a mere month ago. He has been enamored ever since!" Lord Forbes smiled, not showing a trace of his earlier concern.

"And then last week Frederick and your granddaughter became betrothed. My felicitations!" His companion, Lord Elmsbury, chortled. "You will have to call upon me tomorrow for a hunt to celebrate."

His wife doured at the prospect.

"I certainly shall!" Lord Forbes exclaimed.

"'Tis such a shame that Frederick was called away so suddenly. What is a betrothal dinner without the groom?" Lady Elmsbury said in a nasal voice, her eyes gleaming with glee.

Sophie pressed her lips together to stop them from trembling. She took a steadying breath and said in a superior voice, "When Prince George summons, one comes immediately no matter the circumstances. You are so fortunate not to be faced with such a dilemma. Excuse me, I must see to my other guests."

She ignored her grandfather's sharp inhalation and flitted into conversation with the other guests. "What a dreadful storm we had today..." One could always take conversational refuge in the weather.

She smiled gaily throughout dinner; the picture of the exuberant hostess. She was gracious throughout tea with the ladies; tittering at gossip and pretending not to notice Lady Elmsbury's jibes. All the while her mind worked overtime. Perhaps she should cry off the engagement now? Better that than the ignominious scandal that would ensue should these people find out the truth—that they were being deceived.

She shook her head. Frederick would come. He had not meant what he had said.

"Are you perfectly well, my dear?" Lady Elmsbury had managed to sequester Sophie without her noticing. "One would hope that tonight is not setting the tone of your marriage."

"What is a betrothal dinner next to a royal summons? Far better to curry favor there than in this meager company." Sophie's tongue seemed to have escaped its leash again; how Grandfather would berate her later. She sighed, the tension of the last few hours must be getting to her.

"But, my dear," Lady Elmsbury leaned in conspiratorily, "I heard just this morning that the entire palace has been closed in mourning. Some beloved pet of his Majesty died. No one has been granted entry for days." Her lips curled.

Sophie restrained from cursing. News was slow from London, and given Frederick's connections this was the best excuse Grandfather could devise for him not being here. For him abandoning her right before the guests arrived.

"Yes indeed, Frederick was needed to help console the family. Such a hard time." Before Lady Elmsbury could expose the flaw in her logic, Sophie pretended to be called upon by the other ladies.

She sat surrounded by her companions, trying to summon her courage once more. But courage was fleeing with hope and Sophie's responses were faltering.

"Hush, ladies. Becoming a bride is so tiresome, let us leave our hostess to rest," said a friendly face. Sophie could not recall whom.

Some time later, Lord Forbes found Sophie leaden faced in her chair.

"Come, my sweet. He will return when he has calmed himself," he said kindly.

"He said he would never come back. That if we could not agree on a wedding breakfast, that there was no point... no point in-" she burst into tears.

Lord Forbes raised his eyebrows. "The disagreement was that serious? Perhaps we should not have gone forward with the dinner..."

Sophie renewed her sobbing.

"Hush now. No one will find out that we... *embellished* the details of Frederick's whereabouts. He will be back any moment now, and all will be well." His voice was lacking its earlier conviction.

Sophie regained a modicum of control over herself. "Lady Elmsbury knows." She said in a quiet voice.

"That sly shrew... did she mention it to the other guests?"

Sophie shook her head.

"Then she must be planning to embarrass us more publically. If only Lord Elmsbury had some control over her." He said regretfully.

Sophie slumped as much as her stays would allow.

"Do not worry, my sweet. I will fix this." Lord Forbes stood up vigorously and strode out of the room.

Her grandfather had always been good to her. With nothing else to do, Sophie took comfort in his confidence and retired for the evening.

"Are you okay, my lady?"

Sophie shook her head and focused on her maid. "What was that, Daisy?"

"My Lord has been gone for two days. Do you need anything, my lady?" She repeated.

Sophie smiled banally. "You know how Grandfather is. He made plans for a hunt with Lord Elmsbury."

Daisy curtsied and exited the room.

Sophie had barely stepped foot outside of her room when Lord Forbes' valet appeared.

"My lady, may I intrude upon your morning?"

She gestured for Thomas to proceed.

"I did not wish to disgrace Lord Forbes, but... he did not retire after the betrothal dinner. Nor did he leave with a companion."

Sophie's stomach went cold. He had not left to see Lord Elmsbury; now not one man had abandoned her, but two.

"My Lord is a good man, he would not disappear like this. I fear he has been hurt." The butler continued.

Sophie allowed herself a false titter. "How droll of you. Lord Forbes made plans to see Lord Elmsbury."

She waited until Thomas left in relief, then spun on her heel.

"The old fool..." she muttered as she burst into the stable.

Mounting, she proceeded to circle the grounds. She pulled the reins in annoyance as her search proved futile. Grandfather had not gone out for a walk, then. Perhaps..?

She flicked the reins and rode the way he had; the rough path to Frederick's manor. Soon degradation forced her to slow her horse; the storm had washed the meager path away.

"Help!" She knew that cry.

She rode into the trees with speed, her horse expertly picking safe ground. The sight before her made her rein in unnecessarily hard.

He was safe. Lord Forbes was walking stolidly along, pulling his horse behind him.

"Grandfather!" She hurled herself into his arms.

"I am glad to see you, my sweet. Old Kicker is not doing so well," he motioned wearily to his horse.

"Is he lame?"

Lord Forbes shook his head. "Injured, but he should recover if we get the weight off him."

Sophie stepped back from him and noticed the bundle in the saddle for the first time.

A worn face appeared. "Forgive me?"

Hope burst through Sophie's chest. Frederick had never been more dashing.

"I was so filled with despair as I left that I did not notice the damage to the trail. I broke my leg and missed our betrothal dinner."

Relief flooded through Sophie. He had not abandoned her.

"The wedding breakfast does not matter, so long as you will be my wife."

She stepped forward and kissed him soundly on the mouth. Her grandfather let put an ungentlemanly whoop in celebration. She threw her head back and laughed. In that moment, Sophie knew that she was forever blessed, for she had not one man that loved her, but two.

Love Flames Anew

By Michelle Helen Fritz & E. A. Shanniak

H arrison felt as if vicious tiny winged pixies with pitchforks were stabbing him repeatedly in his aching eyes and all along his addled-brain. The incessant drumming of his heartbeat in his ears made him nauseated. He groaned in dismay and nearly fell from his leather-backed chair. Between the pounding drumbeat and the stabbing of the metaphoric pitch-forks, he felt as though his entire head was engulfed in flames.

Nay, 'twas not pixies tormenting me, but little demons with pointy teeth. If only they would tear into my heart and rip it from my body, then mayhap true peace could be found.

Ever so carefully, Harrison turned his head to the side. Between slivers of the dark drapes covering his study's windows, subtle rays of sunlight attempted to invade his sanctuary. He cringed.

What day is it?

Harrison reached for the leather-bound diary which was resting atop his desk at the tips of his long-tapered fingers. He eyed the book with dis-taste as he opened it and leaned back into his chair. An acrid taste filled his mouth as he glanced at his own handwriting and rambling thoughts. Dying fire embers bathed the room in a soft glow. Harrison angled the little book so his eyes could make out his last entry.

Date… I have no conceivable idea.

What a waste this stupid thing is. Why Edmund is so set against me discarding this useless tome is beyond me. Nothing of substance is contained within. I find the idea of keeping an account of my broken heart to be very tiring. For the record, Edmund, I should fire you for your impertinence, but I lack the fortitude to do so. Do not be overly surprised when the day dawns that I chuck this useless thing from the window or mayhap the fireplace would suit as a better resting place.

Harrison ran a hand down his face and his fingers tangled in his beard.

Beard? When had that grown?

His eyes felt gritty and dry, as though bloodshot, and for a moment he wondered when he'd last bathed, much less groomed. Shrugging, he reasoned it didn't signify whatsoever. He had no one to be presentable for. He was the master of this tomb in which he dwelled. Alone. Mr. Lyons, his steward, had been tending to the tenants and his butler was seeing that the staff was being paid. All his responsibilities were being attended to. His presence within the world was of little consequence.

I could die right here and now, and nothing in this world would change so drastically that it would much matter.

Staring off into the dying embers, Harrison let his mind wander to kissable lips and golden hair. Hazel had become his favorite color and his ruination.

Where had I blundered? he wondered for the millionth time. *I paid calls upon her, I took her for rides, I showered the lady with praise and attention, and still… I came up short. I must have done something woeful, said something distasteful, or mayhap it is all of my miserable self combined; because my failings had me passed by for Michaelton, whom I considered to be my friend. How has this happened? Jilted and left all alone. I am ever left alone.*

The study door opened and in blustered his valet, Edmund. "Good afternoon, my lord! The birds are

singing, and the sky is such a beautiful sight this day."
Edmund made his way further into the room and
drew the drapes. Harrison groaned. Unfiltered sunlight streamed into the room as tiny specks of dust
waltzed upon the air.

"I should terminate you!" Harrison bellowed, then
winced as the pain flared within his head.

Seems as if the pixies are content tenants.

"Tsk. Then you would have to miss me, too. We
can't have that happen. 'Tis time to begin your day.
Shall I ring for tea and breakfast?" Edmund strode
to the massive mahogany desk and reached for the
rubbish bin. He began to gather crumpled papers and
empty bottles of spirits to discard.

"That one is not yet empty." Harrison leaned forward and snatched the brandy with a sneer.

"There's nought more than a drop or two remaining," scolded Edmund.

"Every drop is a balm to my soul."

"*Every drop is a nail in your coffin,*" muttered
Edmund, shaking his head at his employer. He
walked to the study door and opened it, placed the
rubbish bin in the hall, and closed it again. "It reeks
in here. We need to air out this room and, I daresay,
you as well. You cannot continue along in this manner,
my lord. What would your esteemed parents say?"

"You can have no idea what they would say. You
never met them," deadpanned Harrison.

"That matters not. I've heard tales. As your con-
fidant, I beseech you to turn your thoughts beyond
this bitter betrayal."

"How am I meant to set this behind me? I loved
her!" Harrison rubbed his chest. "I love her still, and

I shall never have her." Running his tongue over his teeth, he cringed. An unpleasant taste lingered. Swallowing, he choked, then gagged.

Edmund's eyes grew large, and he dashed to a corner table to grab a porcelain vase. He quickly darted back across the room with the vase extended and his face a mask of utter panic as he brought it over for his lordship. When his master stopped heaving into the antique family heirloom, Edmund set it outside of the study alongside the rubbish bin. "Today is a new day, my lord. You can begin anew."

"To what purpose? I have no one, Edmund. I am alone in this world and fear I always shall
be."

"What a load of rubbish! You have your staff, your tenants, and you have the Mortens. Simon has paid a call every day this week and you have turned him away each time, yet he is loyal to you. You have your entire life ahead of you and you are wasting it. You could be doing so much good and yet you are content to rot within this chamber. For, where do you spend your days? In that chair. And where are your nights spent? In that *very same chair*! By goodness, I shall not stand by and aid you any longer! You want to molder in that chair, so be it, but I won't stand by and witness this descent for a moment longer." Edmund strode for the door with his face a mask of outrage.

Harrison wanted to care. He wanted to rise and see to his affairs, but he just wasn't capable of such a feat. His body was weary, and his mind was tired. Sleep eluded him, and those few nights that he fell into slumber were fitful and plagued by nightmares.

He had relied on the brandy to douse his thoughts and calm his mind, for only when he was truly in his cups, could he find peace.

"Wait, please," he tentatively called out.

Edmund stopped with his hand on the door but didn't turn around.

"Have the London papers arrived yet?" Harrison inquired with hesitancy as if he were attempting to find words to say.

"They have."

"I do not believe my eyes at present will allow me to focus upon the words. Would you read it to me?"

Edmund turned around slowly and raised his brows. "If you recall, I tried to read to you the day before and you demanded I take my leave. I'll be glad to read to you, if you can be civil."

Harrison hung his head and felt horrid. Had he not rescued his valet at university from abuse? *And here I am bellowing at him and mistreating him.*

"Forgive me, my friend, I never meant to behave so appallingly."

"I can forgive you anything, my lord, except the ruining of yourself. That I shall no longer accept." Edmund crossed his arms, his stance rigid. His eyes seemed to be focused intently upon the floor under his boots.

"First the paper and perhaps a bath and a shave?" Harrison attempted to sound chipper, but he couldn't keep the glower from his features.

"Very good. I shall ask for some eggs since you haven't consumed anything edible in days." Edmund promptly opened the door and left Harrison to his thoughts.

It had not been easy, this reclaiming of his life and purpose, but he was at least trying. He was reading the newsprint himself and eating what was put before him. He was still drinking here and there, but not to excess. He was riddled with tremors and nausea if he didn't sip from the spirits here and there throughout his day. Harrison was making himself do all manner of things, even though the nightmares persisted. He was far from ready to be entertaining or to be out amongst society, but he was attempting to be a better man, not such a ghost of his former self.

Edmund crept into the study and in his wake trailed Simon. Harrison narrowed his eyes at his valet, who pretended to ignore his irritation as he quickly quit the room. Simon entered further into the study and blinked his eyes. The lighting was dim as Harrison was still in the habit of shying away from the sunlight. The horrid sunbeams beckoned his notice and bid him to venture to the out of doors where life was rife.

Harrison was upset with Edmund for placing him in the position to play host and so he sat as still as a statue. Cold and unmoving. Harrison watched as Simon propped himself into the leather chair before his desk. His friend rested one booted foot upon his knee and jiggled it every so often. For a half hour, they remained locked in the oppressive silence of the room.

When Simon could take no more, he hastily said, "Look here, chap: it can't be *that* bad."

And looking at his young friend who was staring at him with such an honest and open look, Harrison spoke. "I'd been in Town and met a lady. I believed she was attached to me and I courted her with the express purpose of making her my countess. She accepted my pursuit and my gifts. I even traveled back here to fetch mama's ring to make her mine, to give her a token of my affection when I took to bended knee. When I returned to her parent's town-house, Michaelton was there. He beat me to it. She was all smiles and simpering and he was boastfully proud of his coup of stealing her away," Harrison's voice trembled before he cleared his throat, willing his emotions to stay locked away. With impatience at himself, this unmanly display, he shifted in his seat before continuing on. "I was dumbstruck there in the sitting room, attempting to offer congratulations and keep my wounded heart from bleeding all of its pieces upon the carpet before the pair. When I was finally able to make my departure, Samantha followed me to the foyer and confessed that she hoped I was not *too upset*. She tittered and remarked that it wasn't as if we were in love. And blast my stupid tongue, for I told her that for me, every moment, every stolen kiss, every lingering caress had meant a great deal." Harrison took a breath and reached for the decanter of brandy. He poured a fingerful and drank it down, savoring the burn. He wished it could burn the words from his mind and the haunting memories from his heart.

Simon sat forward and balked, "Good God, man! The harpy! You are much better off knowing her true character now. The devil take her and Michaelton!"

He reached for the brandy decanter and stood. He made his way to the liquor cart and selected a glass. He poured himself a decent amount of the amber liquid and set the decanter back down onto the cart. He took a sip and reclaimed his seat.

"Do you know how she greeted my confession?" Harrison quirked a dark brow.

"I am afraid to ask." Simon shook his head.

"She looked at me and replied, 'I do not want *you*! I want what Lord Michaelton can give

me! I never wanted *you*! Why, the idea is ridiculous!' She found my feelings so merry that she laughed." Harrison could always count on Simon to take up his cause and share in any joy or indignation. Simon did not disappoint.

"A pox upon her and her entire house! And Lord Michaelton's! May she plague his heart out! Honestly old chap, you dodged a bullet. Who needs women? They are such a nuisance, except for my sister but she does not signify." Simon waved a hand in the air.

Harrison nodded. He both admired and esteemed Simon's sister. They had all been playmates and Harrison, being an only child, delighted in their companionship. The oldest Morten sibling was away with seminary studies, but Matthew had been great fun too. Many of his most cherished memories had been created with the Morten family at its center. And when his loving parents had been unexpectedly taken from him, 'twas Mr. Morten, the parson, who had consoled him and offered him aid and guidance until his uncle could be by his side.

I have been remiss in my sequestering away from them. When they have lifted me and carried me through time and

*again from despair. What must the youngest of the family
think about my poor behavior? And yet… My heart must
mourn… Am I to never know joy again? Happiness?*

Simon rubbed a finger over his lips before he
spoke, "She misses you, you know. She all but begged
me to bring her along today. Mariah is growing into
quite the beauty, and I fear for the hearts of all the
local country lads."

Mariah has always been so dear to me, but I
turned my attentions in other directions, because
the thought of her ever looking at me as more than a
brotherly figure was unfathomable. How many times
had I allowed my heart to hope that one day, Mariah
might be mine?

"But she would never stoop so low as to break any
of their hearts. She certainly wouldn't find entertainment in such a thing." Harrison took another swig
from his tumbler.

"Right you are! So, we shall only consign the lady
who duped you to Hades. 'Tis time to seek greener
pastures, my friend. You must be out and amongst
society. There are other ladies who are worth your
notice. Let all thoughts of the silly chit flee from your
mind. She did not deserve you."

Harrison felt another smile overtake his face. At
first it was hesitant, and then it morphed into something more. How long had it been since a sincere smile
had formed upon his features? His mood was lighten-
ing within Simon's presence. How was it that a visit
from an old friend could so alter his mood? Simon
could be cavalier in his manners and bordered on the
fringe of impolite in certain situations, but his heart
always meant well. Harrison was blessed to know him.

The two men were content within each other's company, that they didn't exchange many more words thereafter.

When Simon rose to take his leave, Harrison felt sorrow to see him go.

"I am sorry to see you depart. But I shan't be demanding and require you to stay. But mayhap, if you have the time, would you consider returning?" Harrison kept his gaze solidly upon the desk before him. He didn't wish to ascertain what his friend thought of his request, he only desired the knowledge that his friend would be returning.

Before Simon could take another step, he replied, "I give you my word, that I shall come again." He inclined his head toward him.

Simon's declaration did much good to Harrison's mending heart.

True friends are what keeps one going when all seems lost.

Harrison had spent another sleepless night and his humors were foul. He didn't want company and told Edmund to turn Simon away if he paid a call. His mood was darkening again with feelings of self-doubt and loathing. The words of his parents within his nightmares and their faux disappointment with him stalked him at all hours. No matter how he tried to reason and rationalize their harsh accusations away, they refused to leave him be. He felt their disapproval clean to his soul, no matter that it was all in his mind.

In life, his parents had been warm and loving, not the ghouls who unrelentingly haunted him. They had nurtured him and encouraged him in all he undertook. This unrelenting assault upon him stole the warmth and love that his memories usually granted to him.

With Edmund by his side, he had spent the last few days tackling the mountain of correspondence that accumulated. Slowly, order was being restored to his life. He was thankful that in this at least, he was excelling.

A week had not yet passed by when Billingsley, his butler, walked in and announced that Simon had come to pay a call and was accompanied by his sister. Dread filled his being at the thought of such a bright light as Mariah witnessing his current failed state. He at least looked like the lord of the manor now that he was allowing Edmund to dress and groom him again. Truth be told, he felt immensely better being presentable. His state of disarray and surly attitude had frightened more than one maid. But still, still, he was not the man that he'd once been, and he doubted that he could ever be such a cavalier young man again. His makeup had forever been altered.

Harrison took a deep breath and nodded his assent to Billingsley to allow his guests entrance. He should have risen and greeted his guests in the drawing room, but he hoped they would soon take their leave.

No need to be too welcoming…

Simon entered the study first, followed by Mariah. The man had not overstated his sister's blossoming.

Her form had much altered since last they met. *Time marches onward. She is stunning.*

Mariah was now graced with a womanly figure and, while she had always been a beauty, he was knocked for a loop. He would happily plant a facer to any pup who dared look her way. Reining himself in, he reasoned he felt the surge of protectiveness toward her as he had long ago served as her hero in their childhood antics.

I am nothing more than another of her brothers...

He quickly gained his feet and closed the distance between himself and his guests. He

halted before the siblings and bowed at his waist: Simon bowed in return while Mariah executed a perfect curtsey.

Clearing his throat which had gone mysteriously dry, Harrison spoke, "I trust that you are well?" This statement was directed to the lovely woman as he motioned toward the pair of wingback chairs near the fireplace.

"I have been in excellent health, my lord," she said with a blush infusing her lovely complexion.

Harrison discovered that he had no desire to venture far from her side, which wasn't horribly curious as he had always enjoyed her company... But now, he found that he could not break his gaze away from her own intense stare.

What is this bemusement lingering between us?

Billingsley re-entered the room and brought in the tea service, which broke the spell betwixt them. Harrison blinked his eyes as Mariah immediately made her way over to the side table and began to prepare tea for the gentlemen. She remained silent as she served the tea but gave Harrison a brilliant smile that did odd things to his heart. Mariah never needed to be told more than once what was one's preferred way to take their tea, she was such an exceptional hostess. When he had his tea in hand, he watched her softly pad over to the tray and lift a small basket. She returned to his side and pulled aside the covering, showing the contents to him.

"I made these this morning, especially for you, my lord. I do hope lemon is still a favorite of yours." Mariah retrieved a biscuit and gingerly held it out to him.

Harrison took the treat and cast her a small grin. "Still a favorite. Thank you for the trouble you undertook." His heart was acting very bizarrely, and he found this interaction was unsettling him in ways he could not name.

By Jove! What is the matter with me?

Waving her hand in the air she replied, "What trouble? I enjoyed thinking that perhaps my small gift would brighten your day." Then she turned back to the silver tray and picked up her own teacup and saucer.

Simon strode to the drapes and pulled them open with a triumphant, "Huzzah! Now we may pay a proper visit and expel this doom and gloom." Then he took his refreshments to his seat in one of the armchairs before the desk.

Harrison could not spare one word for his friend. His gaze was locked upon Mariah who had taken a seat in the direct sunlight. Her brunette hair was gleaming in the light and her sapphire eyes shone with pleasure.

She still delights in the rays of the sun. And how lovely she is. So like an angel of heaven that has been delivered into that very chair. Why, she is ethereal, otherworldly... A goddess. But she is as a sister to you, old boy. Best to cease these errant thoughts at once. But I'm not making my pulse race, no, that is her, and her alone. And just from the sight of her. Surely, she could never see me as more than just a friend. Lord, is this your prompting? Are you in the midst of working your wonders? Though she is young, she will not always be so. Whether or not you have set her in my path, I shall guard her from afar if I must. It shall be my duty and honor to ensure that she never knows the heartbreak that I have clung to for much too long. I cannot bear to see her suffer, not when I may act as a buffer.

The lady was speaking to him, and he had not heard one word. He cleared his throat, again. "It seems I was woolgathering. What were you saying?"

She beamed at him and said, "I was wondering if you would dine with us tomorrow or perchance, the day after?"

His brows furrowed. He would have to venture out and leave the safety of his estate to do so. While he was unlikely to meet any gossips of the ton, he was hesitant. But when he did not give his acceptance of the invitation within a few moments, he watched her face clear of mirth. She looked at Simon and frowned.

"I would be delighted to join you," he quickly answered. He waited for a sourness to squeeze his insides, but none came. He felt content in his resolve to her well-being and happiness.

"How wonderful! Mama shall be overjoyed. We have all missed you." Her smile was back in place, though she would not meet his eyes.

Does she feel this thing that is lingering between us?

From this moment on, Harrison would stop wallowing in his sorrow and be the man God intended. This visit with his childhood friends was a resounding call to find good, to seek out the light, even in his darkest hours. It was time to let his feelings rest where Samantha was considered. He resolved to never think of her again. Instead, he would endeavor to be a good steward to his tenants and servants, and a better friend to those who welcomed his presence. The Morten family had long taken him under their wings, and he was happy to bask in their warmth in whichever manner he may. If something ever came from this feeling stirring within him toward Mariah, he would rejoice. And if he had to let her go, then so be it. He had always held great affection for her, only now, he wondered if it was morphing into something more.

Was he fickle to move on from thoughts of Samantha to Mariah? What did that say about his character? Was it fickleness that was his greatest downfall? Perhaps an attack of pride? His feelings were so complicated. The two women could not be more different. But how was he to ignore the stirrings of his heart when he had thought the useless organ was never to beat for another? These budding feelings were awakening pieces of himself that his time with Samantha had never touched. It was certainly a quandary, something to ruminate upon at a later date, within the presence of only himself. For now, he would allow God to lead his steps on the path that He desired him to walk and discover the answers as they presented themselves.

"I am sorry to be remiss in my duties upon the family of Morten," he teased. He was feeling as light as a feather.

"I suppose, just this once, you may be forgiven," she allowed with a delightful tease coloring her tone.

Harrison bowed his head at her. "I thank you for your many kindnesses."

He realized that Simon was poking about at his bookshelves and the sight was curious to him. When had Simon ever willingly perused books? Still, he felt grateful his friend was allowing this playful turn of the conversation. If he could suss out what her feelings were for him, he would know how to proceed. Perhaps there was hope for him after all. Something more to rejoice in. Mayhap this ending of one love could lead him to the grandest of all loves. One that would last. He would wait and bide his time. He would treat the lady with the respect and kindness that she deserved and perchance, in time, his heart would heal. Any favor, any task he could see to for her would be readily undertaken. He would shelter her when she needed, and he would encourage her when she faltered. He would treasure every encounter and see if things would evolve from there. Because no matter what the future held for her, his greatest wish was for a love that lasts. For both of them.

Would you like to be whisked away to Brighton and witness what happens next to Harrison and Mariah? Love At Last is a full-length novel and is available on Amazon and in KU

You Again

By Ravin Tija Maurice

The mouth of the cave loomed ahead, at least twice my height and wider than my arms could stretch. Normally I would turn away, but I needed the coin.

When deciding to hire me, the magistrate had mentioned past the glob of tobacco he chewed, "Quite the stash to score."

As though I were only tempted by riches.

With a dismissive snort, the magistrate added, "Should be easy for a former Red Cloak like you."

Clearly, he'd never fought a troll.

Behind me, I recognized the sound of gravel crunching under foot and branches snapped. A creak of leather, followed by a chink of metal. Sounds of some one, not *some thing*, creeping up behind me rather than trying to inch it's way forward from the darkness ahead. Fingers on the hilt of my sword, I whipped around, drawing my blade.

"You again!" I stared down the length of an all too familiar longsword, eventually connecting with a pair of bright blue eyes fixed intently on me.

He chuckled as we made eye contact, lowering his weapon. "Keep popping up like this, and I might think you're following me." He approached, his eyes on the mouth of the cave for signs of movement. "Since when do the Red Cloaks take an interest in local monster issues?"

I looked away, my feet shifting back and forth, blade still drawn but lowered. In my defense he still carried his weapon. "They don't."

"You're disobeying orders?"

"I've parted ways with the Red Cloaks." I sheathed my sword, avoiding eye contact with him.

"Finally taking my advice?"

"They are corrupt to their core, like a rotten apple. They're not what I believed them to be."

He sheathed his sword and stood shoulder to shoulder with me, eyes turned towards the cave. "What do you say we do this together? Split the bounty?"

"Why, Lord Greythorne, are you proposing we become partners?"

He held out a leather clad hand. Although he didn't smile, his beautiful blue eyes twinkled with mischief. "For now, then we'll see how it goes. I suspect we will have competition. We have a better chance succeeding together."

I shrugged. "That's alright with me, but are you sure you can keep up?" Punching him in the shoulder with a laugh, I started walking into the cave.

We crept along in the darkness, keeping close to the cave walls. The wide cave mouth gave off a fair amount of light, helping guide us along although we kept in the shadows. He always stayed within arm's reach. Not that I *needed* him, but I enjoyed his company. Sure, he was handsome and charming, but he could hold his own in a fight and knew how to use his sword, no pun intended. And his sword had prominence; called Saving Grace, the magical sword was used to slay the witchling that almost destroyed the planet.

If you were the type who believed in legends.

Hand on hilt, ears perked for sound, eyes adjusting to the growing darkness, I whispered, "You never told me how you came into possession of a sword with such history."

A rumbling echoed ahead of us.

We both stopped.

His arm encircled my waist and pulled me to him as he flung us against the wall.

I didn't stop him. Keeping alive was a high priority. We kept still and silent as we waited, listening, watching.

Nothing. With the coast momentarily clear, I exhaled in relief. His breath on my neck made my skin tingle. Perhaps it was the looming potential danger, that moment of dire possibility, or his arm still around my waist, but I found myself smiling, leaning into him, his chest plate cold and firm against my back. Turning my head so our cheeks touched, I raised my hand to stroke the soft stubble on his jawline. My eyes closed for a brief moment, remembering past thoughts of passion with this man.

Sebastian Lammond, Lord Greythorne, was good, honorable and loyal.

I wasn't any of those things. *Yet.* But I wanted to be. Would he ever want someone like me? I could hope.

"Shall we pretend death approaches and make love against this wall?" He asked in my ear, the soft hairs of his stubble tickling my cheek.

"Have we got time?" We stood together as the rumbling continued.

My hand went to my small crossbow I kept strapped to my hip. I knew, even though I couldn't see, his other hand was on the hilt of the sword.

"Remember trolls can smell your fear," he whispered.

"I am not afraid." I pulled away from him but held tightly to his hand as we continued to walk forward. Losing track of him in this darkness seemed foolish, and it also gave me an excuse to keep hold of his hand.

"I'm assuming fear sweat smells differently. Or trolls possess some magical ability."

I snorted. "In my experience, trolls are *not* magical."

Something farther into the cave heard me and copied the sound, its much louder snort echoing off the walls. He laughed. With him behind me, I could not see the smile that accompanied the laugh, but the thought of it was enough to spread warmth through my chest.

A loud bang from outside the cave startled us both. We turned in tandem to face the entrance. Far enough away that we were shielded by darkness, but not enough that we needed to light a torch to see clearly, there were no signs of anyone else. Catching a glimpse of light, I noticed a tunnel just to the left of where we came in. Having to battle other hunters on top of a troll didn't appeal to me one bit.

Before I could say anything to Sebastian we heard another bang, this time from further inside the cave. Too late, we realized the troll heard the same sound we did. From a ways deeper into the dark, heavy footsteps thundered, shaking the world around us as the ten-foot-tall troll came running out of the black, ready to protect its home. I almost felt guilty for hunting it, almost, then remembered its favored snack was the femurs of young children.

"Do we wait it out or follow?" I asked Sebastian.

"If you want to collect the bounty, we must return with evidence," he said. "Evidence of the body parts nature. Head, feet, teeth, hands. Any or all."

I sighed. "They wouldn't simply trust you at your word? I figured *Lord Greythorne* carried a certain amount of…what's the word I'm looking for?"

"Oddly enough, no." He drew his sword from its sheath. Uttering a few words beneath his breath, the blade radiated blue, infused with magical energy. It cast a small amount of light around us, giving his face an eerie glow.

I gestured towards the split in the cave ahead as I drew my crossbow. "You go right. I'll go left."

He nodded, his eyes already on the right side. I didn't mention that I wanted to avoid bumping into any Red Cloaks unprepared so I was being cautious.

I hesitated, wanting to say more, but what was there to say? Wish him luck? Beg him to stay with me? Another offer of a quick romp? For all I knew, this could be the last time I saw him, although I had more faith in both our abilities than to let fear shake my resolve. Swallowing against all the things I wished to say to him and all the things I doubted he wanted me to say, I turned towards the smaller tunnel on the left.

As I stepped forward, his hand caught my arm.

"Wait," he commanded.

My heart leapt into my chest, assuming it was another instinctual move, an act of protection. Then he pulled me to him. Releasing my arm, he captured my waist again, this time to pull me against his chest.

"Be careful, Ashlyn," he said, then bowed his head low to kiss me.

Eyes wide, a gurgle of surprise in the back of my throat, it took the tightening of his arm about me to realize what was happening. My only regret was having only one free hand to snake around his neck as I welcomed the embrace.

Hope. A sign he felt as I did. A sign we were meant for greater things. All that fear and indecision washed away with one perfect kiss.

He released me, our eyes locking on each other. With a wordless squeeze of my hand, he conveyed his earlier sentiment.

"You too, Sebastian."

Clearing my thoughts of Sebastian, I started down the tunnel left, watching and listening. Darkness closed in around me, but I continued to push forward, trying to keep a steady pace despite not being able to see anything except the exit.

Noises echoed ahead. I followed the sound — a scuffle? The tunnel lightened as it curved, and before I'd taken a hundred steps, I spied the forest ahead, a second entrance to the cave. Either I had taken the wrong tunnel and Sebastian was now fighting the troll on his own, or....

Pushing my way through a large bush blocking the entrance, the forest floor came into view. I blanched. Remnants of body parts littered the ground, blood sprayed around like a rainfall.

Human parts.

The earth shook. I wrinkled my nose at troll stench. Lo and behold, there it stood to the right of the cave-mouth, surveying its handy work, having quickly dispatched whoever crossed its path before me. With no time to inspect the debris, I silently prayed it wasn't Sebastian. Gnashing its broken teeth, spittle dripping from its maw, the troll roared. I almost stumbled back, deafened. I silently thanked a deity

I didn't quite believe in that I wasn't wearing red; trolls, like several other monsters, *hated* the color red. I learned the hard way a few times.

Smirking, I called out, "Hey, big boy! Wanna make all this real easy?"

The ground shook as it ran at me. I shot a bolt from my crossbow and hit him in the left eye. With an deafening scream, it stumbled, swiping its arms in front.

Saving Grace glinted in my peripheral. With deft skill, Sebastian swung his blade, striking the troll's leg, blood spraying around it. The troll yipped and yowled in pain, grabbing small trees, yanking them out of the ground and pelting them in the direction of me and Sebastian.

Looks like we pissed it off. But then, I'd be angry too if a puny human shot out my eye with an arrow.

Sebastian dodged. First an uprooted tree. Then a shower of bits of rocks.

I reached for a new bolt to reload.

The troll snarled, spittal flying. Its putrid smell wafted towards me, and I stopped myself from gagging.

My hand stalled when I saw the troll's mitt grapple a boulder, watching the ground split as it yanked it free. Bolt in one hand, crossbow in the other, I darted forward.

Zig zag. One way, then the other. Must be a challenging target for the troll-turned-cyclops.

Ducking behind a tree, I reloaded.

Squeak as the bow stretched.

Click as the bolt locked.

Thunk as my body yanked against the tree trunk.

Around my waist was not the warm embrace of Sebastian's protective arm but the gnarled hand of the troll. My scream died in my throat as the hand wrenched me free.

My crossbow slipped and clattered to the ground below. The world spun. The hand squeezed.

My lungs flamed and my limbs creaked as the hand tightened its hold. Any tighter and the bones in my arms would snap like twigs. Red clouded my vision as the troll shook me.

With my dying breath, I yelled, "A little help!"

A rib popped. Then another. Fire irons of pure pain, my screams like forced squeaks as I gasped for air.

Now or never.

My cry for help must not have been heard. Sebastian was not coming to my rescue.

Now or never.

Wriggling my fingers, I worked to free my arms, ignored the fear of dislocation, and fought for my life. One hand free. Then another. As the world spun and another fire iron stabbed, I drew the dagger I kept sheathed on my left wrist. I stabbed the small blade in at each of its finger joints, hoping the pain would help loosen its grip.

Maybe. Just maybe.

A glint of the sun hitting metal causes me to squint, and Saving Grace came swooping down and struck the troll in the shoulder. I only caught a glimpse of Sebastian's face as the troll yowled in pain, tossing me to the side, discarded.

The world spun and spun as I flew up and through the air, before slamming hard into a tree. The wind knocked out of me when I slid down and hit the ground. The loud crack I heard hopefully wasn't my spine.

When my face hit the dirt, light exploded in my eyes and the world didn't stop its gut-wrenching spin before everything went black.

There was movement around me before the world came back into view. Rustling, thumping, slicing, and a blood curdling howl as Sebastian Lammond, Lord Greythorne, dispatched the troll with his magical legendary blade, Saving Grace. Surely the bards would sing about this one.

The world came back into view as his familiar face appeared above me.

"Did we get him?" My grizzly voice asked. I sounded like I'd been smoking a dwarf pipe.

Sebastian laughed. "Yeah, we got him."

"When you say we, you mean me, right? I consider the crossbow bolt in the eye what turned the battle in our favor. And my back isn't broken. I take that as a win."

Sebastian chuckled as I tried to sit up. "I suppose you helped a little."

Before I could protest, he pulled me onto his lap.

"Once we collect our bounty, we will go home so you can heal." He examined my expression. "We'll pick up your gear too."

"Home?"

"Greythorne manor. Home." His face went a little pink with blush. "You did mention something about partners, I figured it's as good a place as any to have as a home base. Or do you have your eye on...."

"Shhh." I stretched my arm up, grabbing the front of his chest plate as if I grabbed his collar, and pulled him close so I could kiss him. His long blonde hair must have come undone during the fight as it fell around his face, framing it perfectly.

"I thought you'd never ask."

A Note from Paullett Golden

Dear Reader,

Thank you for reading this collection of short fiction. If you're interested in learning more about the authors featured in this book, read their bios in the next few pages, and follow their provided social accounts where applicable.

This collection offered short fiction exclusively. If you're interested in exploring this type of fiction further, check out my blog: https://www.paullettgolden.com/post/flash-fiction-writing

Supporting indie writers who brave self-publishing is important and appreciated. I humbly request you review this book on Amazon with an honest opinion. Reviewing elsewhere is additionally much appreciated.

One way to support writers you've enjoyed reading, indie or otherwise, is to share their work with friends, family, book clubs, etc. Lend books, share books, exchange books, recommend books, and gift books. If you especially enjoyed a writer's book, lend it to someone to read in case they might find a new favorite author in the book you've shared.

All the best,
Paullett Golden

About Paullett Golden

Celebrated for her complex characters, realistic con-
flicts, and sensual portrayal of love, Paullett Golden
writes historical romance for intellectuals. Her novels,
set primarily in Georgian England, challenge the
genre's norm by starring characters loved for their
imperfections and idiosyncrasies. The writing aims
for historical immersion into the social mores and
nuances of Georgian England. Her plots explore
human psyche, mental and physical trauma, and personal convictions. Her stories show love overcoming
adversity. Whatever our self-doubts, *love will out*.

Paullett Golden completed her post-graduate
work at King's College London, studying Classic

British Literature. Her Ph.D. is in Composition and Rhetoric, her M.A. in British Literature from the Enlightenment through the Victorian era, and her B.A. in English. Her specializations include creative writing and professional writing. She has served as a University Professor for nearly three decades and is a seasoned keynote speaker, commencement speaker, conference presenter, workshop facilitator, and writing retreat facilitator.

As an ovarian cancer survivor, she makes each day count, enjoying an active lifestyle of Spartan racing, powerlifting, hiking, antique car restoration, drag racing, butterfly gardening, competitive shooting, and gaming. Her greatest writing inspirations, and the reasons she chose to write in the clean historical romance genre, are Jane Austen, Charlotte Brontë, and Elizabeth Gaskell.

Connect online
paullettgolden.com
facebook.com/paullettgolden
twitter.com/paullettgolden
instagram.com/paullettgolden

About Michelle Helen Fritz

Michelle Helen Fritz began her literary career as a personal assistant to Indie authors. She enjoys being immersed in the process of turning an idea into a complete and published book. Michelle loves to write about dashing heroes and the compelling women that tempt them with a bit of intrigue and an abundance of romance, creating swoon-worthy characters and stories for her readers to enjoy. Occasionally, her characters talk to her and change the entire plot. Maryland is where her humble abode resides, housing her four home-schooled children along with her jaunty hero-husband who makes all her dreams come true. Michelle fully believes in happily-ever-afters and wishing upon stars.

Connect online

Facebook: https://www.facebook.com/
Author-Michelle-Helen-Fritz-111085181423828/

Instagram: https://instagram.com/
authormichellehelenfritz

Bookbub: https://www.bookbub.com/
authors/michelle-helen-fritz

About Abbie Grubb

Abbie Lynn Grubb lives in Texas with her husband and son, two dogs, and two cats. She is an Army brat who loves traveling, reading, baking, and spending time with family and friends. She is a college history professor by day and a historical fiction and romance author by night. Her favorite books are those that celebrate friendships, whether they are romantic or platonic, and she enjoys a good tale of an epic quest now and then as well. When not juggling classes, PTO, or cub scouts, she enjoys nothing more than being at home with her family.

About H.J. Palmer

Hannah is twenty-four and lives in regional NSW, Australia. She lives with her husband and their two sons, as well as the family's pet dog, Rocky. When she is not wiping a bum or being overwhelmed by testosterone, Hannah is working on her novels and reading anything that she can get her hands on. She attributes all credit to God, coffee, and her husband, who kindly watches the kids while she writes.

About Ravin Tija Maurice

Ravin Tija Maurice is a multi-genre author from Ontario, Canada. Her works range from historical to the not-so-distant future; some with paranormal elements, some with sci-fi, but all featuring strong female leads.

"You Again" is her first romantic fantasy, with more to come!

She's also a mother, reader, stuffed animal collector, tabletop gamer and hobbyist.

She loves talking to readers and fellow writers! Come say hi!

Connect online
Insta - @prophecygirl13
Twitter - @heartbamboo

www.facebook.com/RTMaurice
www.tiktok.com/@authorravintmaurice
www.authorravintmaurice.weebly.com

About E.A. Shanniak

E.A. (Ericka Ashlee) Shanniak is the author of several
successful series: A Castre World Novel – Whitman
Series Western Romance – Dangerous Ties Series. She
is hobbit-sized, barely reaching over five feet tall on a
good day. When she wears her Ariat boots, not only
does she gain an inch, she is then able to reach the
kitchen cabinets to get all the snacks. When not in her
fox den of a writing cave, Ericka loves to spend time
with her family – outside having campfires, camping,
fishing, or zooming in the family jeep to another mid-
west adventure. Ericka loves all the animals her kids
bring home including numerous barn cats and their
newfound bantam chicken named Strip. Ericka is an
emergency 911 dispatcher residing in the small town
of Coldwater, Kansas with her wonderful husband,

two amazingly smart kids, and whatever animals her kids bring home this week. You're welcome to follow her on her Kansas adventures with these social media platforms listed below. And please leave a review if you liked what you read. Have a wonderful day!

Connect online
http://www.eashanniak.com/